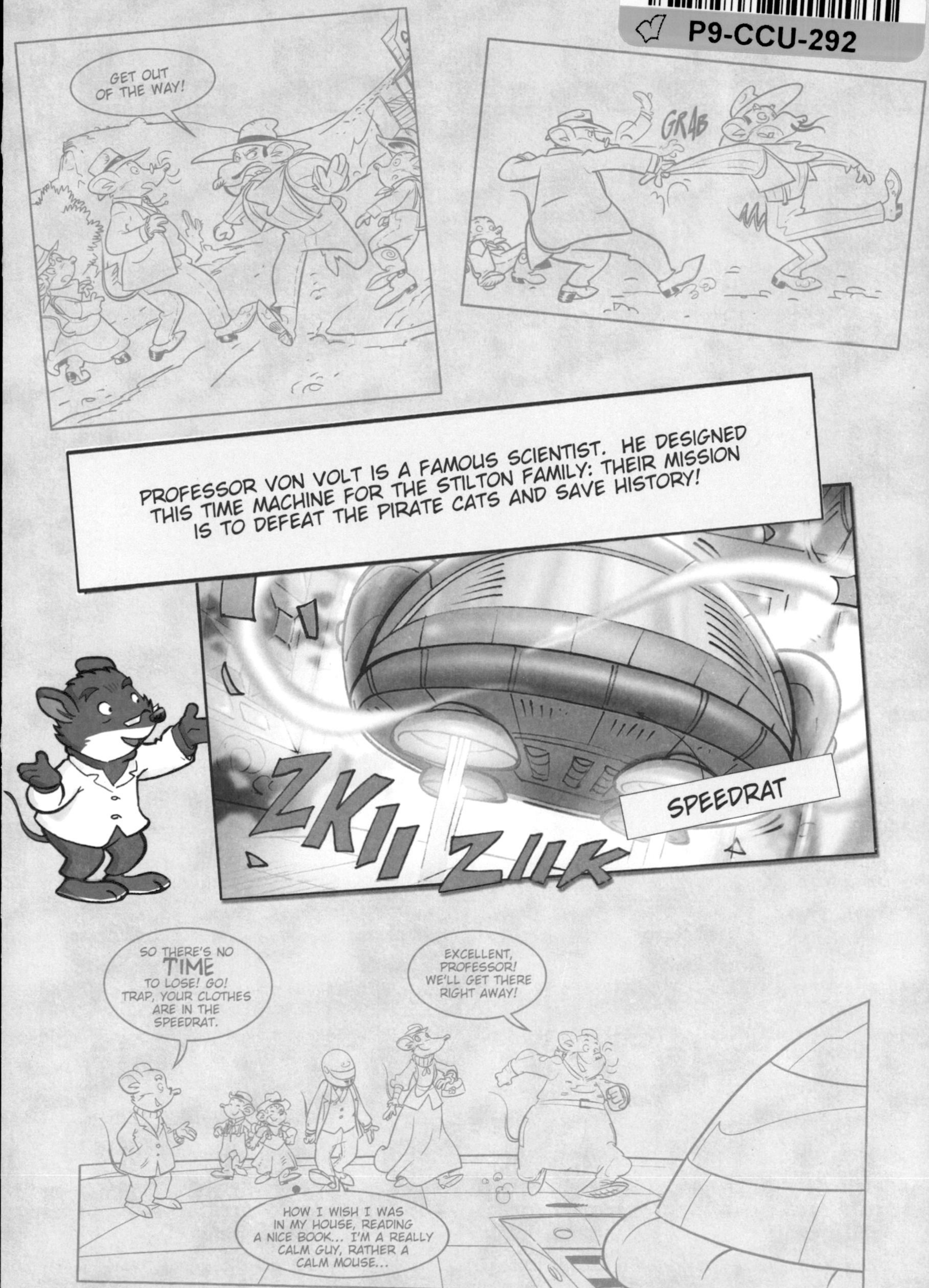
GET OUT OF THE WAY!
GRAB
PROFESSOR VON VOLT IS A FAMOUS SCIENTIST. HE DESIGNED THIS TIME MACHINE FOR THE STILTON FAMILY: THEIR MISSION IS TO DEFEAT THE PIRATE CATS AND SAVE HISTORY!
SPEEDRAT
ZKIIZIIK
SO THERE'S NO TIME TO LOSE! GO! TRAP, YOUR CLOTHES ARE IN THE SPEEDRAT.
EXCELLENT, PROFESSOR! WE'LL GET THERE RIGHT AWAY!
HOW I WISH I WAS IN MY HOUSE, READING A NICE BOOK... I'M A REALLY CALM GUY, RATHER A CALM MOUSE...

Geronimo Stilton

PAPERCUTZ™

Geronimo Stilton & Thea Stilton

GRAPHIC NOVELS AVAILABLE FROM PAPERCUTZ™
...ALSO AVAILABLE WHEREVER E-BOOKS ARE SOLD!

#1 "The Discovery of America"

#2 "The Secret of the Sphinx"

#3 "The Coliseum Con"

#4 "Following the Trail of Marco Polo"

#5 "The Great Ice Age"

#6 "Who Stole The Mona Lisa?"

#7 "Dinosaurs in Action"

#8 "Play It Again, Mozart!"

#9 "The Weird Book Machine"

#10 "Geronimo Stilton Saves the Olympics"

#11 "We'll Always Have Paris"

#12 "The First Samurai"

#13 "The Fastest Train in the West"

#14 "The First Mouse on the Moon"

#15 "All for Stilton, Stilton for All!"

#16 "Lights, Camera, Stilton!"

#1 "The Secret of Whale Island"

#2 "Revenge of the Lizard Club"

#3 "The Treasure of the Viking Ship"

#4 "Catching the Giant Wave"

papercutz.com

Geronimo Stilton

THE FASTEST TRAIN IN THE WEST
By Geronimo Stilton

NEW YORK

THE FASTEST TRAIN IN THE WEST
© 2012 EDIZIONI PIEMME S.p.A.
Corso Como 15, 20145,
Milan, Italy
Graphics and Ilustrations © Atlantyca Entertainment S.p.A. 2012
Geronimo Stilton names, characters and related indicia are copyright,
trademark and exclusive license of Atlantyca S.p.A.
All rights reserved.
The moral right of the author has been asserted.

Text by Geronimo Stilton
Editorial coordination by Patrizia Puricelli
Artistic coordination by BAO Publishing
Story by Michele Foschini
Script by Leonardo Favia
Illustrations by Ennio Bufi
Color by Mirka Andolfo
Cover by Marta Lorini
Based on an original idea by Elisabetta Dami

© 2013 – for this work in English language by Papercutz.

Original title: "Il Treno Piú Veloce Del Far West"

www.geronimostilton.com

Stilton is the name of a famous English cheese. It is a registered trademark of the Stilton Cheese
Makers' Association. For more information go to www.stiltoncheese.com

No part of this book may be stored, reproduced or transmitted in any form or by any means,
electronic or mechanical, including photocopying, recording, or by any information storage
and retrieval system, without written permission from the copyright holder. FOR INFORMATION
PLEASE ADDRESS ATLANTYCA S.p.A.
Via Leopardi 8 20123 Milan Italy –foreignrights@atlantyca.it - www.atlantyca.com

Nanette McGuinness – Translation
Big Bird Zatryb – Lettering & Production
Beth Scorzato – Production Coordinator
Michael Petranek – Editor
Jim Salicrup
Editor-in-Chief

ISBN: 978-1-59707-448-3

Printed in China.
February by WKT Co. LTD.
3/F Phase 1 Leader Industrial Centre
188 Texaco Road, Tsuen Wan, N.T.
Hong Kong

Papercutz books may be purchased for business or promotional use. For information on bulk purchases
please contact Macmillan Corporate and Premium Sales Department at (800) 221-7945 x5442.

Distributed by Macmillan
Third Papercutz Printing

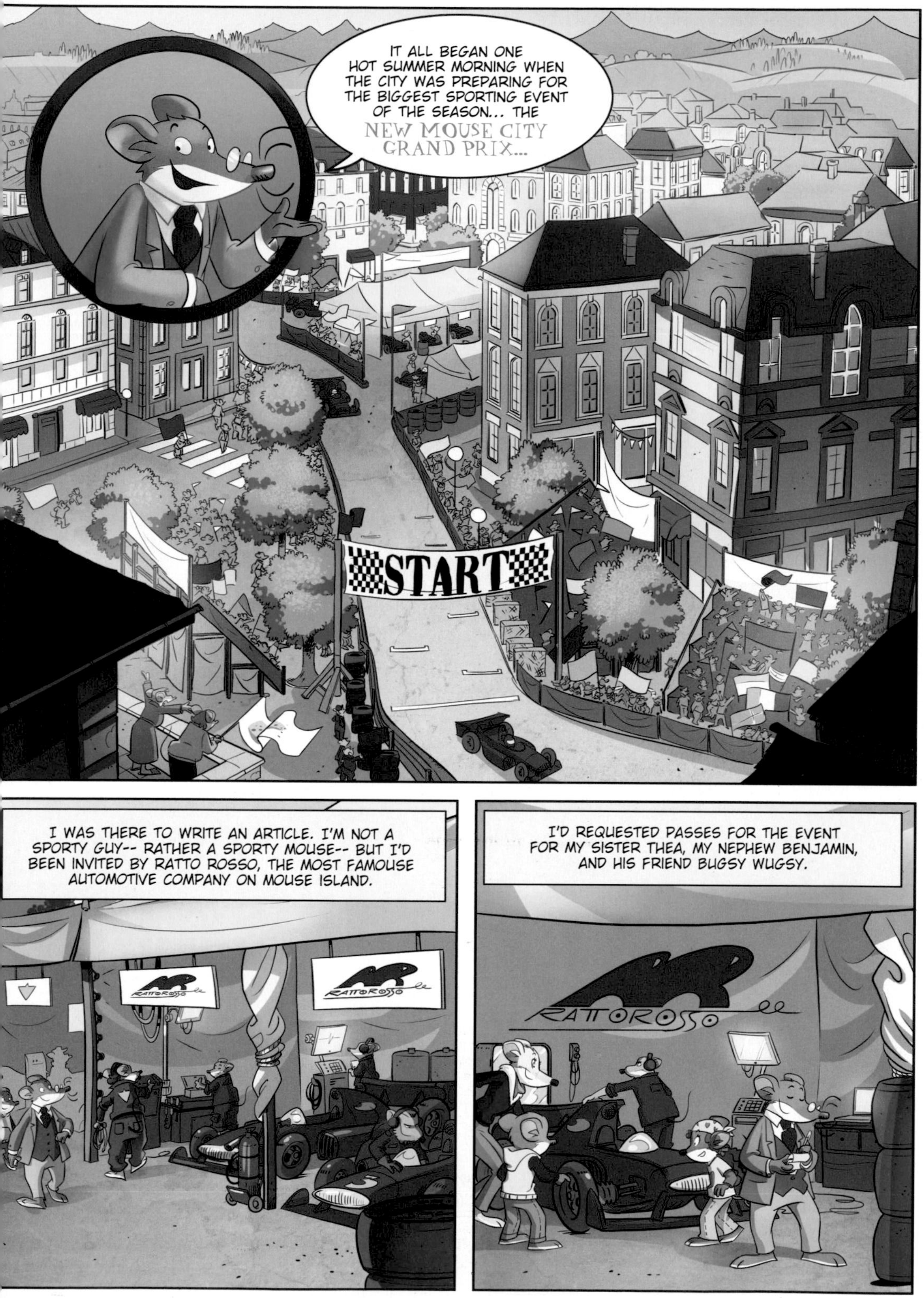
IT ALL BEGAN ONE HOT SUMMER MORNING WHEN THE CITY WAS PREPARING FOR THE BIGGEST SPORTING EVENT OF THE SEASON... THE NEW MOUSE CITY GRAND PRIX...
START
I WAS THERE TO WRITE AN ARTICLE. I'M NOT A SPORTY GUY-- RATHER A SPORTY MOUSE-- BUT I'D BEEN INVITED BY RATTO ROSSO, THE MOST FAMOUSE AUTOMOTIVE COMPANY ON MOUSE ISLAND.
RATTOROSSO
RATTOROSSO
I'D REQUESTED PASSES FOR THE EVENT FOR MY SISTER THEA, MY NEPHEW BENJAMIN, AND HIS FRIEND BUGSY WUGSY.
RATTOROSSO

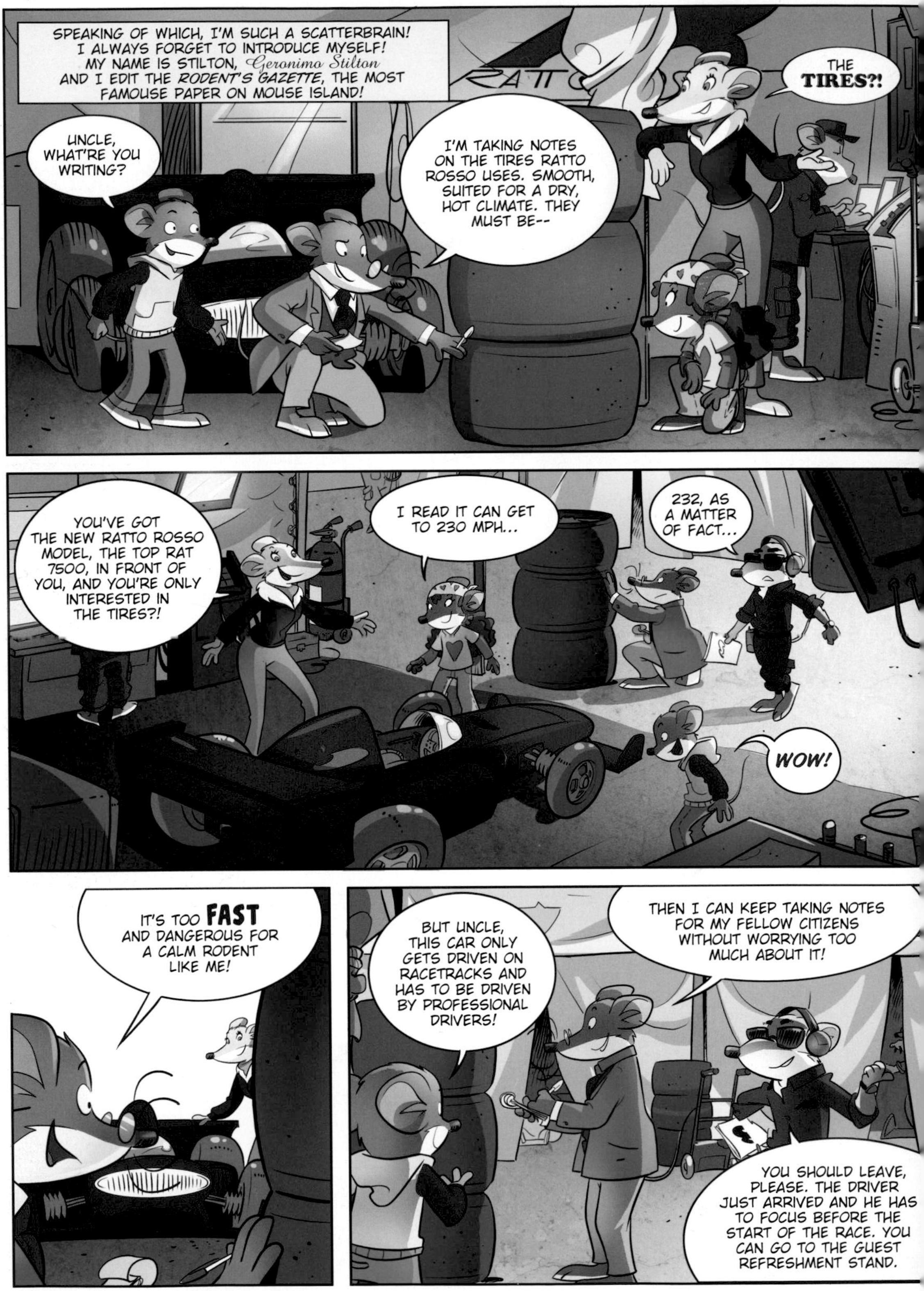
SPEAKING OF WHICH, I'M SUCH A SCATTERBRAIN! I ALWAYS FORGET TO INTRODUCE MYSELF! MY NAME IS STILTON, Geronimo Stilton AND I EDIT THE RODENT'S GAZETTE, THE MOST FAMOUSE PAPER ON MOUSE ISLAND!
UNCLE, WHAT'RE YOU WRITING?
I'M TAKING NOTES ON THE TIRES RATTO ROSSO USES. SMOOTH, SUITED FOR A DRY, HOT CLIMATE. THEY MUST BE--
THE TIRES?!
YOU'VE GOT THE NEW RATTO ROSSO MODEL, THE TOP RAT 7500, IN FRONT OF YOU, AND YOU'RE ONLY INTERESTED IN THE TIRES?!
I READ IT CAN GET TO 230 MPH...
232, AS A MATTER OF FACT...
WOW!
IT'S TOO FAST AND DANGEROUS FOR A CALM RODENT LIKE ME!
BUT UNCLE, THIS CAR ONLY GETS DRIVEN ON RACETRACKS AND HAS TO BE DRIVEN BY PROFESSIONAL DRIVERS!
THEN I CAN KEEP TAKING NOTES FOR MY FELLOW CITIZENS WITHOUT WORRYING TOO MUCH ABOUT IT!
YOU SHOULD LEAVE, PLEASE. THE DRIVER JUST ARRIVED AND HE HAS TO FOCUS BEFORE THE START OF THE RACE. YOU CAN GO TO THE GUEST REFRESHMENT STAND.

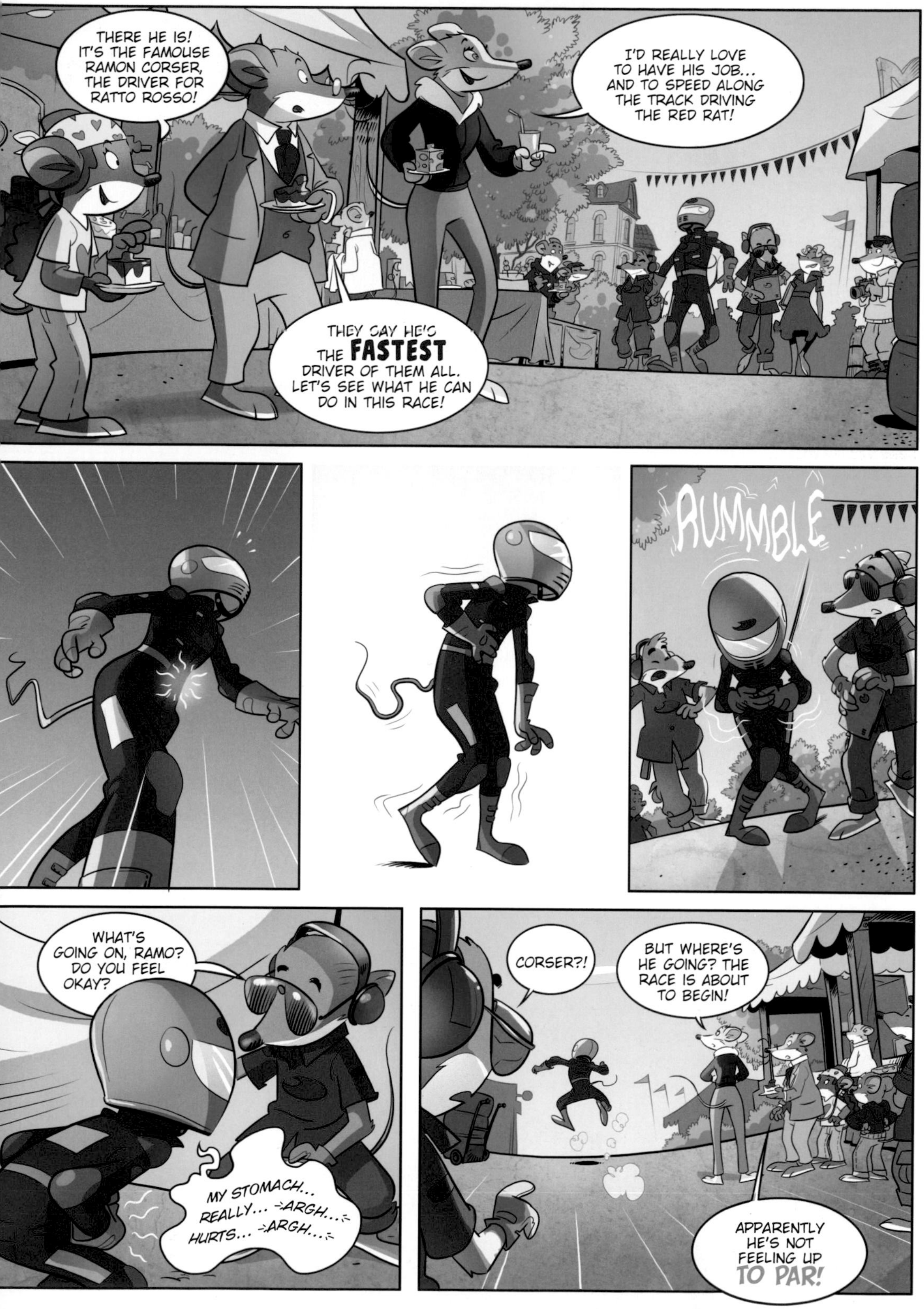
THERE HE IS! IT'S THE FAMOUSE RAMON CORSER, THE DRIVER FOR RATTO ROSSO!
I'D REALLY LOVE TO HAVE HIS JOB... AND TO SPEED ALONG THE TRACK DRIVING THE RED RAT!
THEY SAY HE'S THE FASTEST DRIVER OF THEM ALL. LET'S SEE WHAT HE CAN DO IN THIS RACE!
RUMMBLE
WHAT'S GOING ON, RAMO? DO YOU FEEL OKAY?
MY STOMACH... REALLY... ARGH... HURTS... ARGH...
CORSER?!
BUT WHERE'S HE GOING? THE RACE IS ABOUT TO BEGIN!
APPARENTLY HE'S NOT FEELING UP TO PAR!

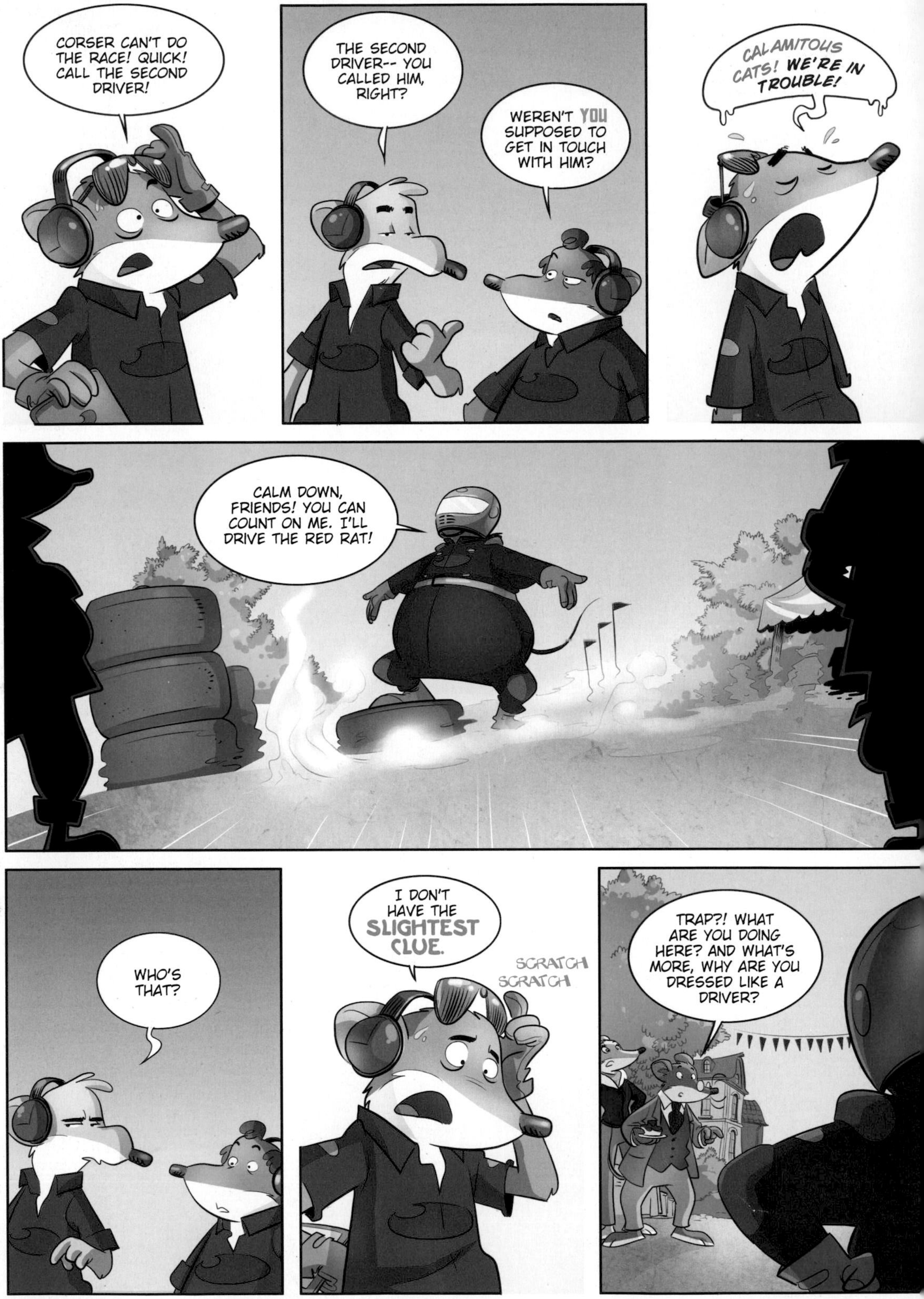
CORSER CAN'T DO THE RACE! QUICK! CALL THE SECOND DRIVER!
THE SECOND DRIVER-- YOU CALLED HIM, RIGHT?
WEREN'T YOU SUPPOSED TO GET IN TOUCH WITH HIM?
CALAMITOUS CATS! WE'RE IN TROUBLE!
CALM DOWN, FRIENDS! YOU CAN COUNT ON ME. I'LL DRIVE THE RED RAT!
WHO'S THAT?
I DON'T HAVE THE SLIGHTEST CLUE.
SCRATCH SCRATCH
TRAP?! WHAT ARE YOU DOING HERE? AND WHAT'S MORE, WHY ARE YOU DRESSED LIKE A DRIVER?

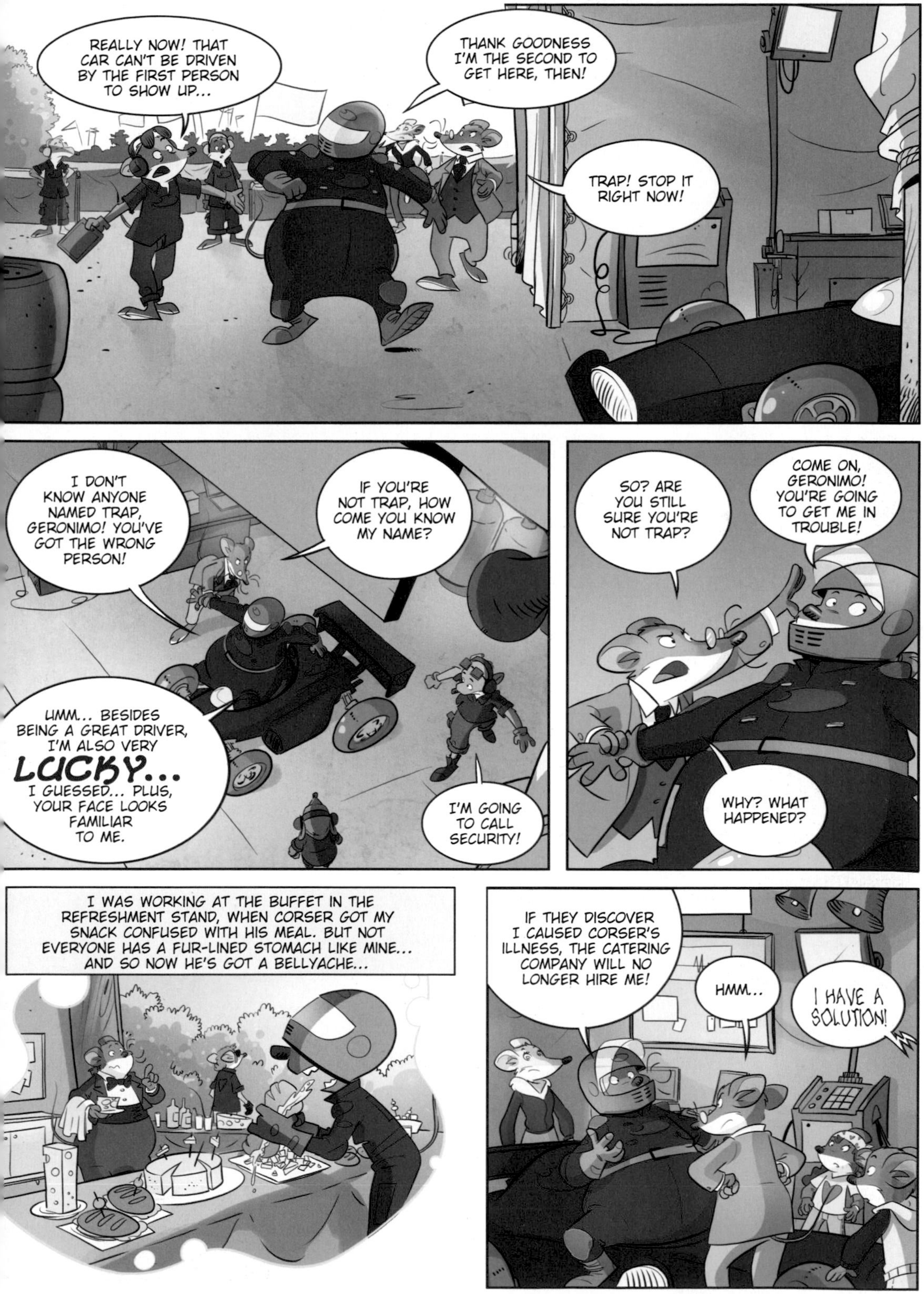
REALLY NOW! THAT CAR CAN'T BE DRIVEN BY THE FIRST PERSON TO SHOW UP...
THANK GOODNESS I'M THE SECOND TO GET HERE, THEN!
TRAP! STOP IT RIGHT NOW!
I DON'T KNOW ANYONE NAMED TRAP, GERONIMO! YOU'VE GOT THE WRONG PERSON!
IF YOU'RE NOT TRAP, HOW COME YOU KNOW MY NAME?
UMM... BESIDES BEING A GREAT DRIVER, I'M ALSO VERY LUCKY... I GUESSED... PLUS, YOUR FACE LOOKS FAMILIAR TO ME.
I'M GOING TO CALL SECURITY!
SO? ARE YOU STILL SURE YOU'RE NOT TRAP?
COME ON, GERONIMO! YOU'RE GOING TO GET ME IN TROUBLE!
WHY? WHAT HAPPENED?
I WAS WORKING AT THE BUFFET IN THE REFRESHMENT STAND, WHEN CORSER GOT MY SNACK CONFUSED WITH HIS MEAL. BUT NOT EVERYONE HAS A FUR-LINED STOMACH LIKE MINE... AND SO NOW HE'S GOT A BELLYACHE...
IF THEY DISCOVER I CAUSED CORSER'S ILLNESS, THE CATERING COMPANY WILL NO LONGER HIRE ME!
HMM...
I HAVE A SOLUTION!

IT REALLY SEEMS LIKE YOU COULD USE A PAW, MY FRIENDS!

P-PROFESSOR VON VOLT?

HELLO, GERONIMO!

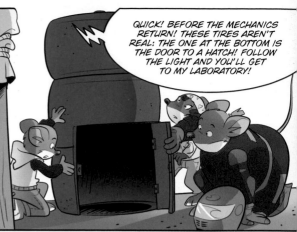

QUICK! BEFORE THE MECHANICS RETURN! THESE TIRES AREN'T REAL: THE ONE AT THE BOTTOM IS THE DOOR TO A HATCH! FOLLOW THE LIGHT AND YOU'LL GET TO MY LABORATORY!

PROFESSOR, HOW'D YOU MAKE AN ENTRANCE TO THE LAB FROM HERE, TOO?

HEE! HEE! HEE! I DESIGNED THE TOP RAT 7500!

THEN YOU COULD'VE MADE IT A BIT MORE CONVENIENT!

IT'S JUST A WHISKER AWAY... FROM WHAT I SAW ON THE MONITOR, YOU WERE IN REAL **TROUBLE!**

MY COUSIN ALWAYS HAS THE ABILITY TO GET HIMSELF INTO A MESS-- RIGHT, TRAP?

PROFESSOR, DID YOU JUST CALL US TO HELP US OUT OR HAS SOMETHING HAPPENED?

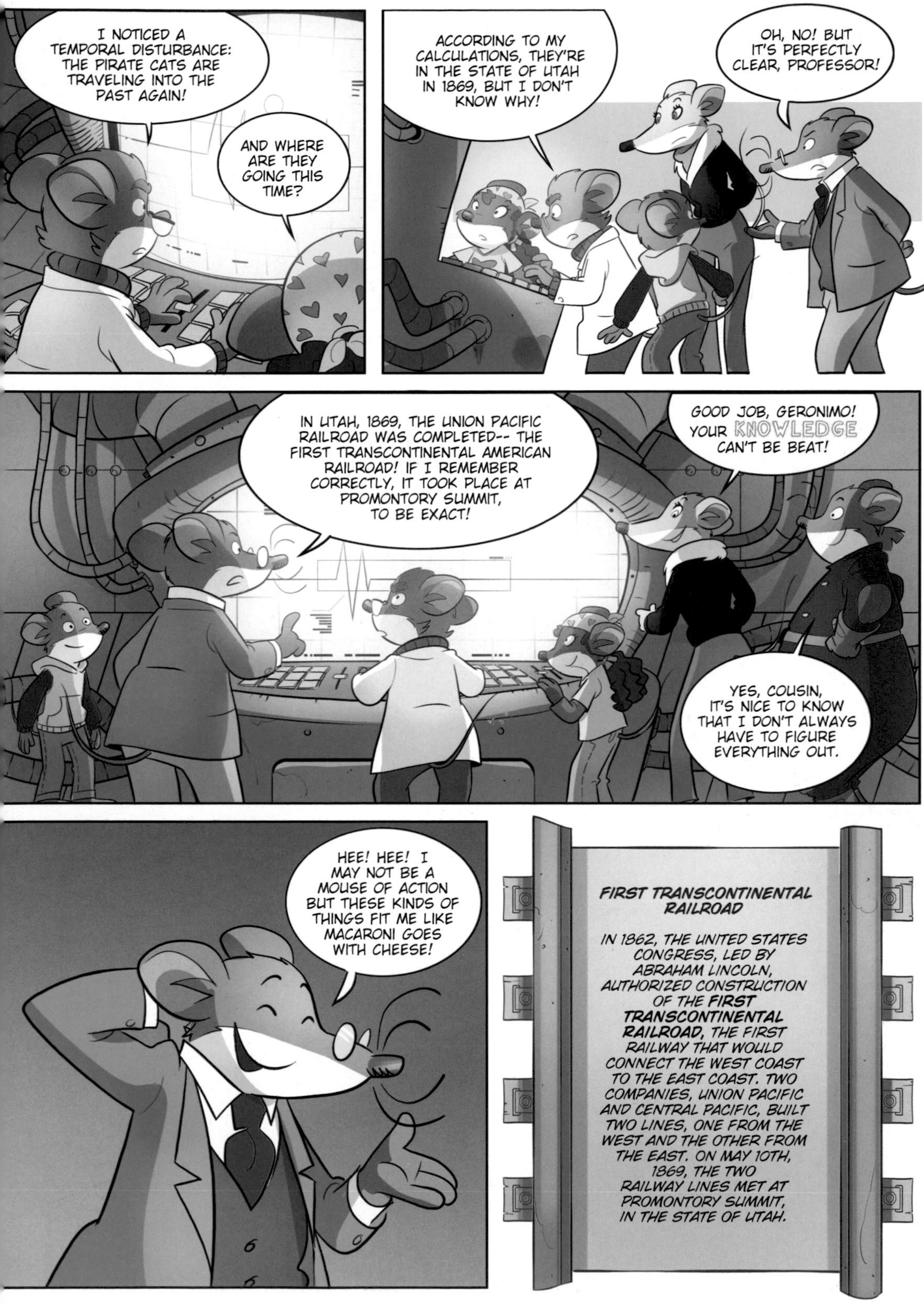
I NOTICED A TEMPORAL DISTURBANCE: THE PIRATE CATS ARE TRAVELING INTO THE PAST AGAIN!
AND WHERE ARE THEY GOING THIS TIME?
ACCORDING TO MY CALCULATIONS, THEY'RE IN THE STATE OF UTAH IN 1869, BUT I DON'T KNOW WHY!
OH, NO! BUT IT'S PERFECTLY CLEAR, PROFESSOR!
IN UTAH, 1869, THE UNION PACIFIC RAILROAD WAS COMPLETED-- THE FIRST TRANSCONTINENTAL AMERICAN RAILROAD! IF I REMEMBER CORRECTLY, IT TOOK PLACE AT PROMONTORY SUMMIT, TO BE EXACT!
GOOD JOB, GERONIMO! YOUR KNOWLEDGE CAN'T BE BEAT!
YES, COUSIN, IT'S NICE TO KNOW THAT I DON'T ALWAYS HAVE TO FIGURE EVERYTHING OUT.
HEE! HEE! I MAY NOT BE A MOUSE OF ACTION BUT THESE KINDS OF THINGS FIT ME LIKE MACARONI GOES WITH CHEESE!
FIRST TRANSCONTINENTAL RAILROAD
IN 1862, THE UNITED STATES CONGRESS, LED BY ABRAHAM LINCOLN, AUTHORIZED CONSTRUCTION OF THE FIRST TRANSCONTINENTAL RAILROAD, THE FIRST RAILWAY THAT WOULD CONNECT THE WEST COAST TO THE EAST COAST. TWO COMPANIES, UNION PACIFIC AND CENTRAL PACIFIC, BUILT TWO LINES, ONE FROM THE WEST AND THE OTHER FROM THE EAST. ON MAY 10TH, 1869, THE TWO RAILWAY LINES MET AT PROMONTORY SUMMIT, IN THE STATE OF UTAH.

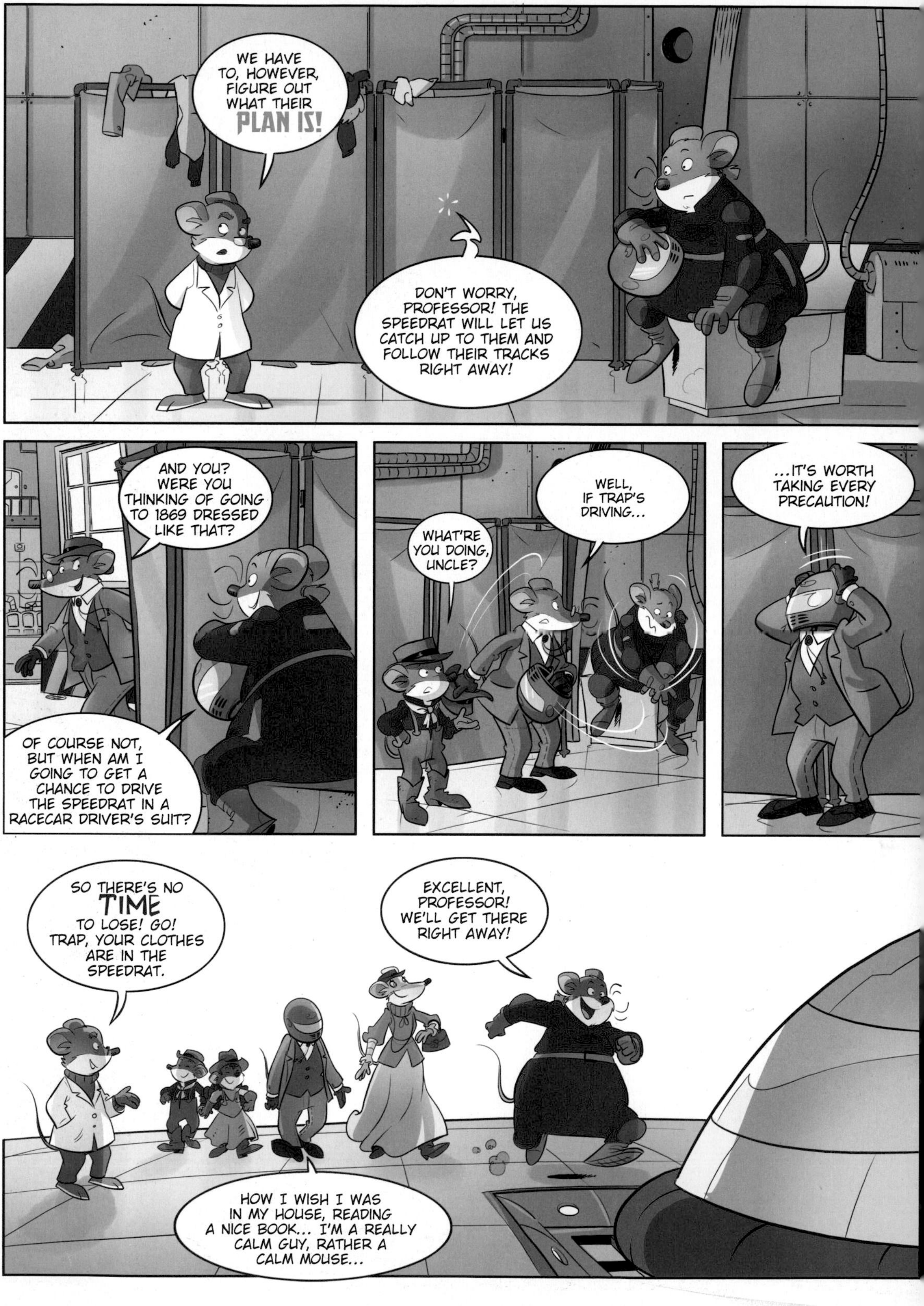
WE HAVE TO, HOWEVER, FIGURE OUT WHAT THEIR PLAN IS!
DON'T WORRY, PROFESSOR! THE SPEEDRAT WILL LET US CATCH UP TO THEM AND FOLLOW THEIR TRACKS RIGHT AWAY!
AND YOU? WERE YOU THINKING OF GOING TO 1869 DRESSED LIKE THAT?
OF COURSE NOT, BUT WHEN AM I GOING TO GET A CHANCE TO DRIVE THE SPEEDRAT IN A RACECAR DRIVER'S SUIT?
WHAT'RE YOU DOING, UNCLE?
WELL, IF TRAP'S DRIVING...
...IT'S WORTH TAKING EVERY PRECAUTION!
SO THERE'S NO TIME TO LOSE! GO! TRAP, YOUR CLOTHES ARE IN THE SPEEDRAT.
EXCELLENT, PROFESSOR! WE'LL GET THERE RIGHT AWAY!
HOW I WISH I WAS IN MY HOUSE, READING A NICE BOOK... I'M A REALLY CALM GUY, RATHER A CALM MOUSE...

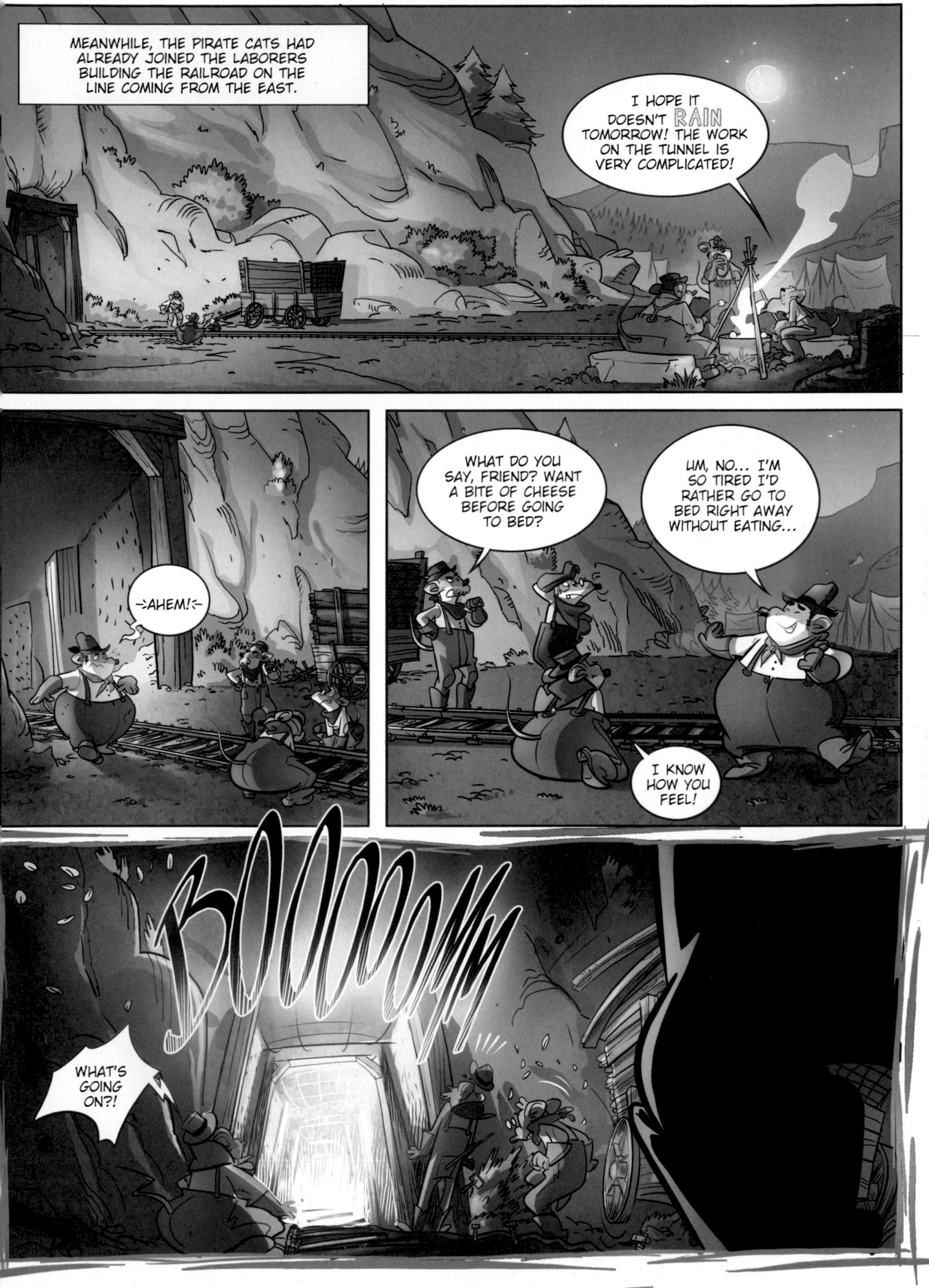
MEANWHILE, THE PIRATE CATS HAD ALREADY JOINED THE LABORERS BUILDING THE RAILROAD ON THE LINE COMING FROM THE EAST.
I HOPE IT DOESN'T RAIN TOMORROW! THE WORK ON THE TUNNEL IS VERY COMPLICATED!
AHEM!
WHAT DO YOU SAY, FRIEND? WANT A BITE OF CHEESE BEFORE GOING TO BED?
UM, NO... I'M SO TIRED I'D RATHER GO TO BED RIGHT AWAY WITHOUT EATING...
I KNOW HOW YOU FEEL!
BOOOOOM
WHAT'S GOING ON?!

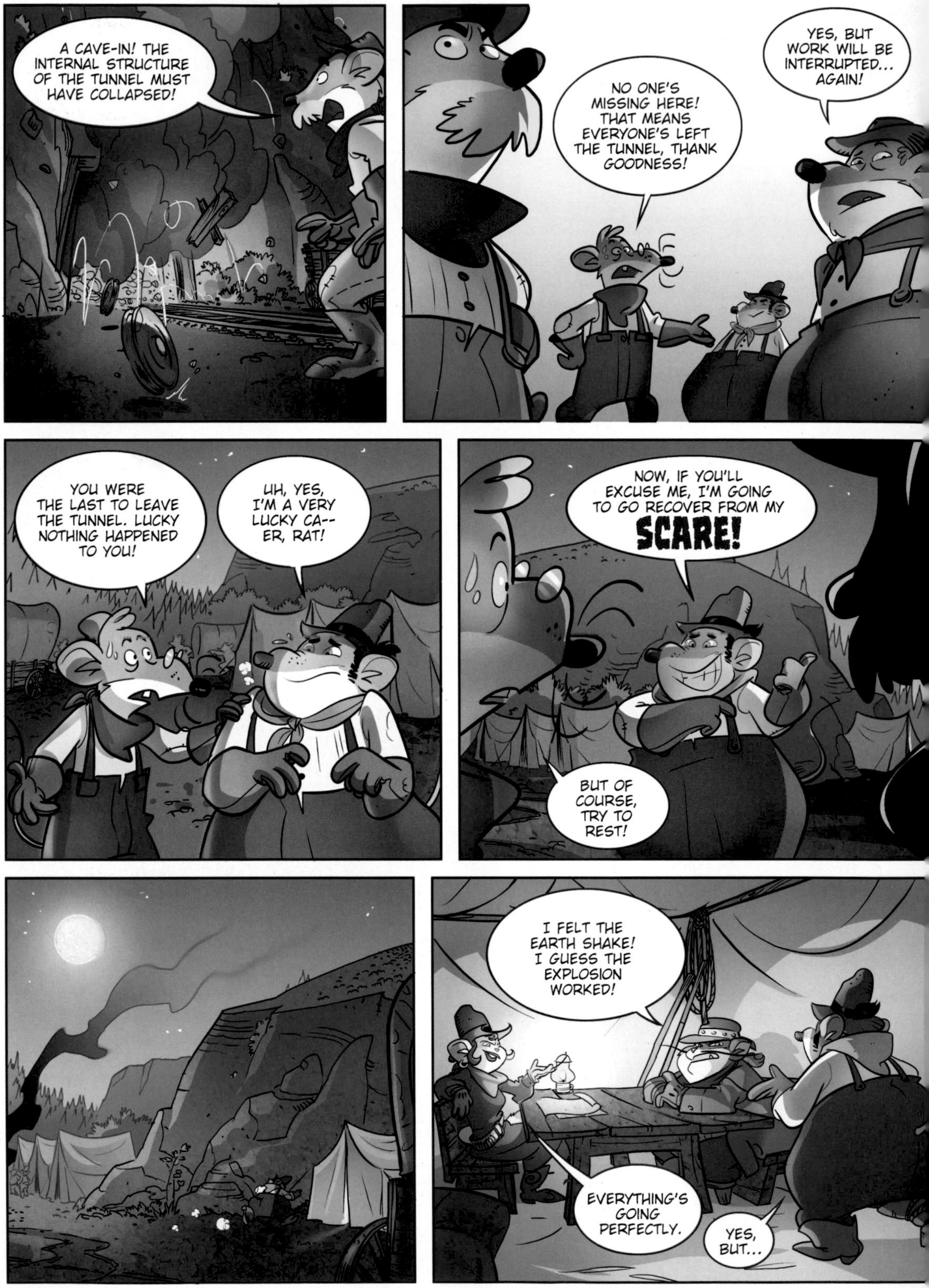
A CAVE-IN! THE INTERNAL STRUCTURE OF THE TUNNEL MUST HAVE COLLAPSED!
NO ONE'S MISSING HERE! THAT MEANS EVERYONE'S LEFT THE TUNNEL, THANK GOODNESS!
YES, BUT WORK WILL BE INTERRUPTED... AGAIN!
YOU WERE THE LAST TO LEAVE THE TUNNEL. LUCKY NOTHING HAPPENED TO YOU!
UH, YES, I'M A VERY LUCKY CA-- ER, RAT!
NOW, IF YOU'LL EXCUSE ME, I'M GOING TO GO RECOVER FROM MY SCARE!
BUT OF COURSE, TRY TO REST!
I FELT THE EARTH SHAKE! I GUESS THE EXPLOSION WORKED!
EVERYTHING'S GOING PERFECTLY.
YES, BUT...

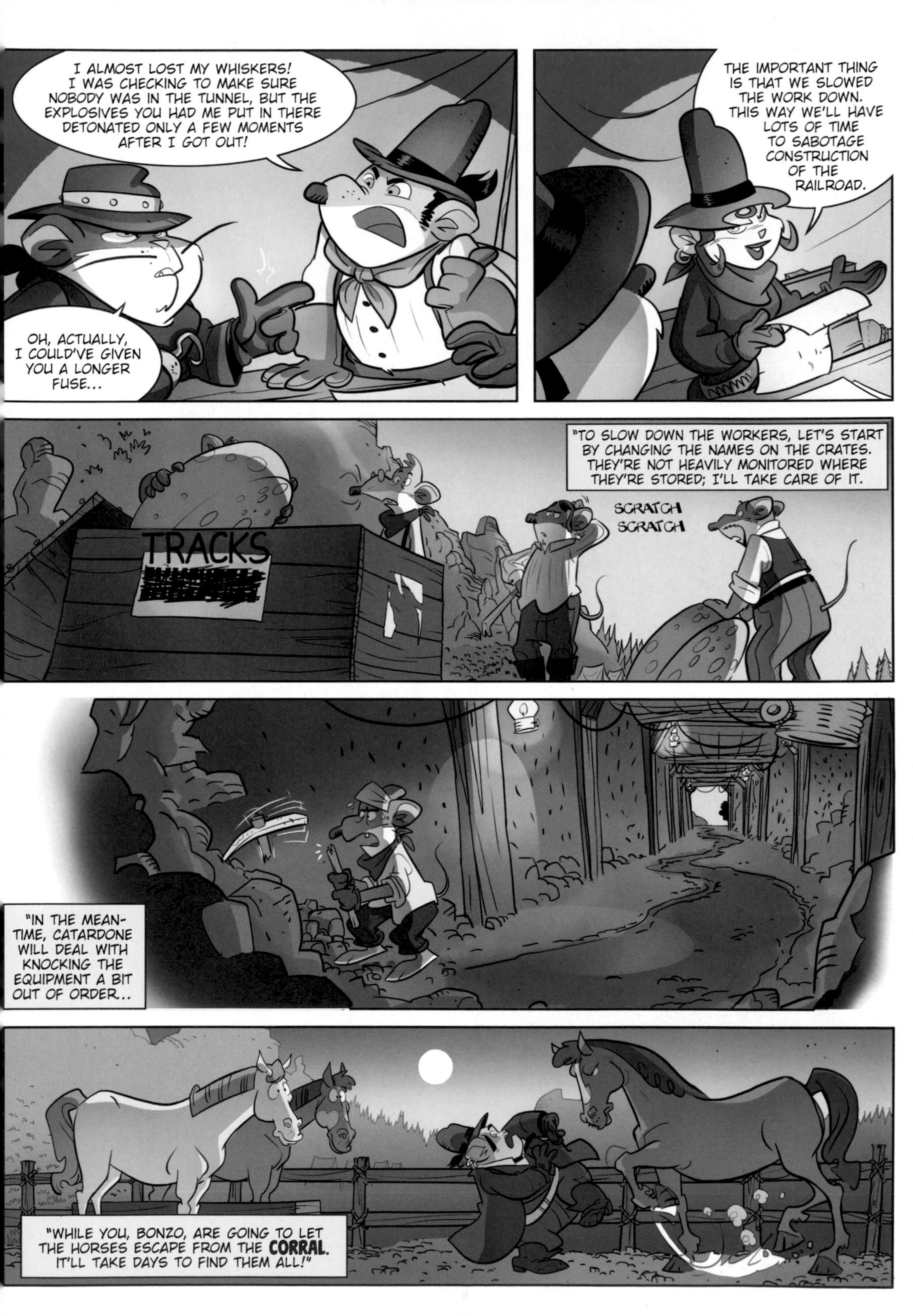
I ALMOST LOST MY WHISKERS! I WAS CHECKING TO MAKE SURE NOBODY WAS IN THE TUNNEL, BUT THE EXPLOSIVES YOU HAD ME PUT IN THERE DETONATED ONLY A FEW MOMENTS AFTER I GOT OUT!
OH, ACTUALLY, I COULD'VE GIVEN YOU A LONGER FUSE...
THE IMPORTANT THING IS THAT WE SLOWED THE WORK DOWN. THIS WAY WE'LL HAVE LOTS OF TIME TO SABOTAGE CONSTRUCTION OF THE RAILROAD.
"TO SLOW DOWN THE WORKERS, LET'S START BY CHANGING THE NAMES ON THE CRATES. THEY'RE NOT HEAVILY MONITORED WHERE THEY'RE STORED; I'LL TAKE CARE OF IT.
TRACKS
SCRATCH SCRATCH
"IN THE MEAN-TIME, CATARDONE WILL DEAL WITH KNOCKING THE EQUIPMENT A BIT OUT OF ORDER...
"WHILE YOU, BONZO, ARE GOING TO LET THE HORSES ESCAPE FROM THE **CORRAL**. IT'LL TAKE DAYS TO FIND THEM ALL!"

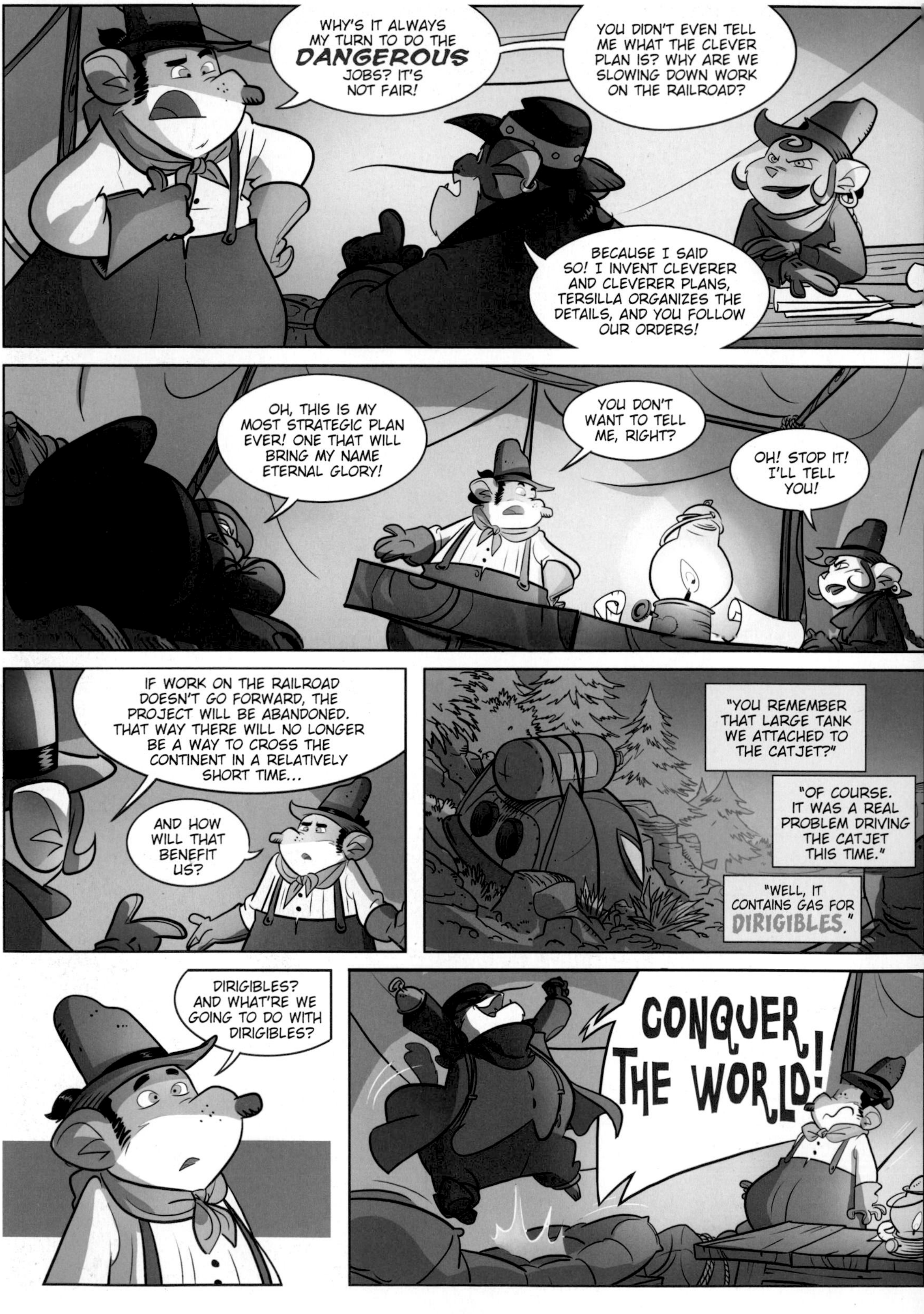

WHY'S IT ALWAYS MY TURN TO DO THE DANGEROUS JOBS? IT'S NOT FAIR!
YOU DIDN'T EVEN TELL ME WHAT THE CLEVER PLAN IS? WHY ARE WE SLOWING DOWN WORK ON THE RAILROAD?
BECAUSE I SAID SO! I INVENT CLEVERER AND CLEVERER PLANS, TERSILLA ORGANIZES THE DETAILS, AND YOU FOLLOW OUR ORDERS!
OH, THIS IS MY MOST STRATEGIC PLAN EVER! ONE THAT WILL BRING MY NAME ETERNAL GLORY!
YOU DON'T WANT TO TELL ME, RIGHT?
OH! STOP IT! I'LL TELL YOU!
IF WORK ON THE RAILROAD DOESN'T GO FORWARD, THE PROJECT WILL BE ABANDONED. THAT WAY THERE WILL NO LONGER BE A WAY TO CROSS THE CONTINENT IN A RELATIVELY SHORT TIME...
AND HOW WILL THAT BENEFIT US?
"YOU REMEMBER THAT LARGE TANK WE ATTACHED TO THE CATJET?"
"OF COURSE. IT WAS A REAL PROBLEM DRIVING THE CATJET THIS TIME."
"WELL, IT CONTAINS GAS FOR DIRIGIBLES."
DIRIGIBLES? AND WHAT'RE WE GOING TO DO WITH DIRIGIBLES?
CONQUER THE WORLD!

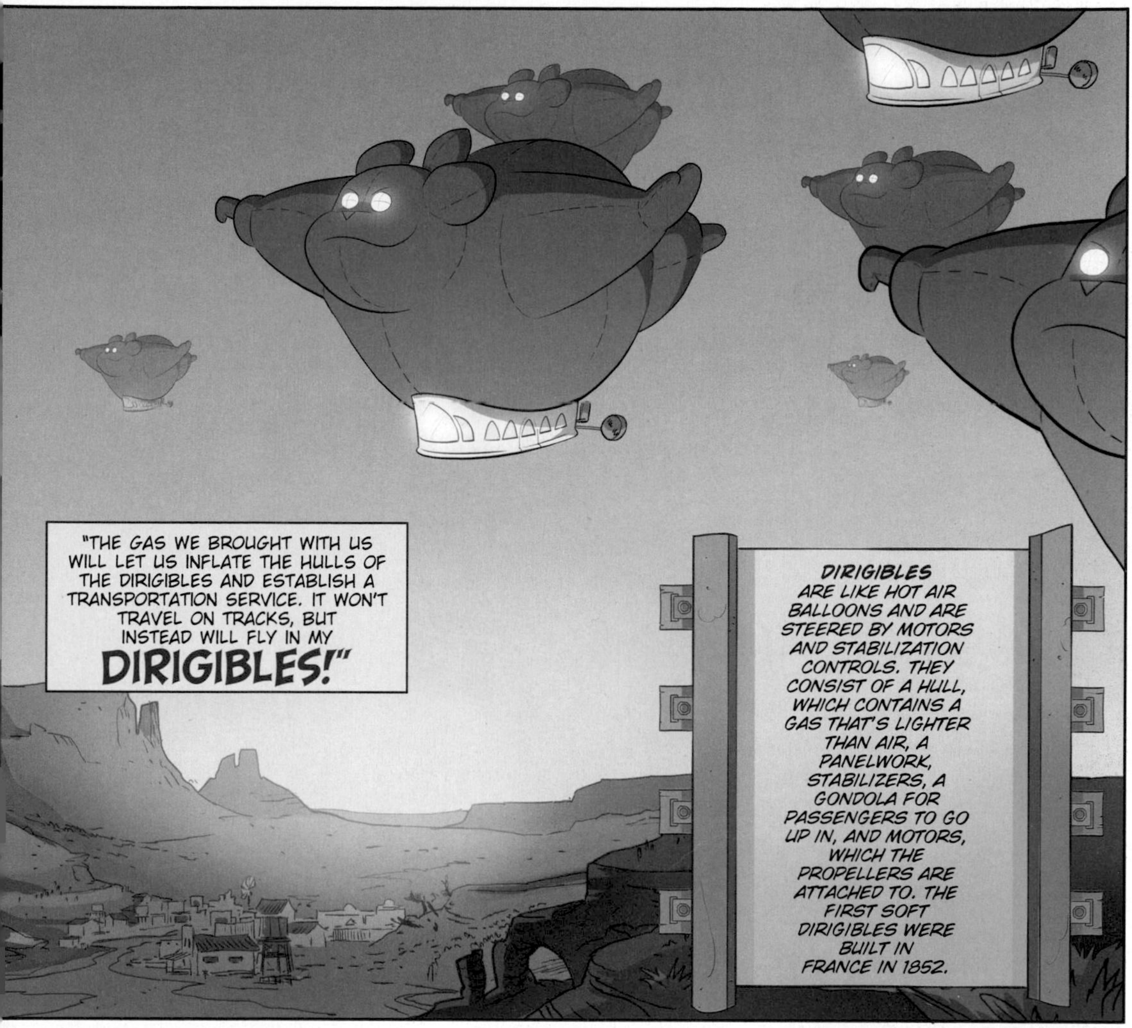
"THE GAS WE BROUGHT WITH US WILL LET US INFLATE THE HULLS OF THE DIRIGIBLES AND ESTABLISH A TRANSPORTATION SERVICE. IT WON'T TRAVEL ON TRACKS, BUT INSTEAD WILL FLY IN MY DIRIGIBLES!"
DIRIGIBLES ARE LIKE HOT AIR BALLOONS AND ARE STEERED BY MOTORS AND STABILIZATION CONTROLS. THEY CONSIST OF A HULL, WHICH CONTAINS A GAS THAT'S LIGHTER THAN AIR, A PANELWORK, STABILIZERS, A GONDOLA FOR PASSENGERS TO GO UP IN, AND MOTORS, WHICH THE PROPELLERS ARE ATTACHED TO. THE FIRST SOFT DIRIGIBLES WERE BUILT IN FRANCE IN 1852.

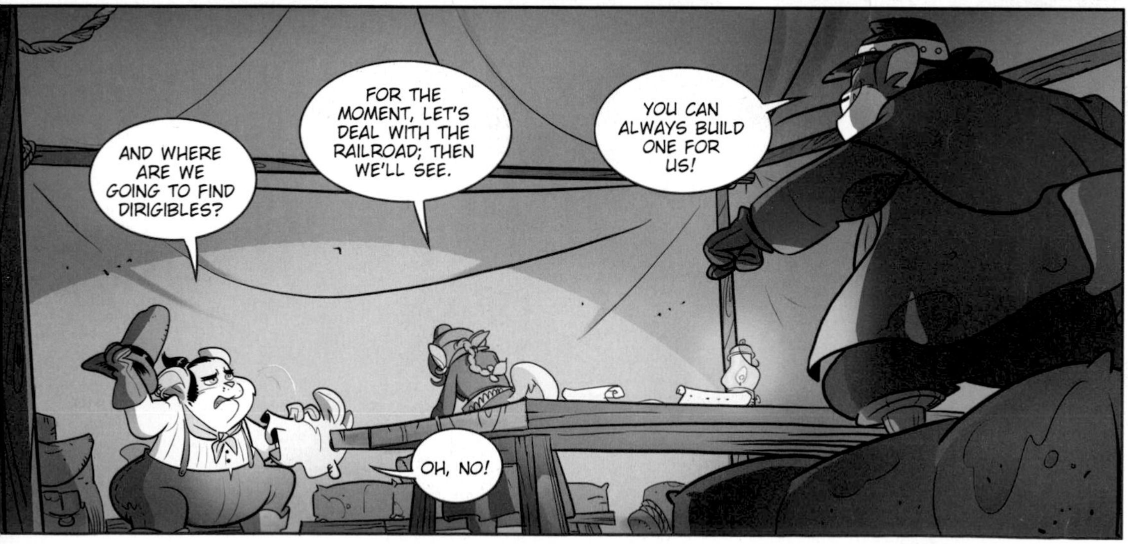
AND WHERE ARE WE GOING TO FIND DIRIGIBLES?
FOR THE MOMENT, LET'S DEAL WITH THE RAILROAD; THEN WE'LL SEE.
YOU CAN ALWAYS BUILD ONE FOR US!
OH, NO!

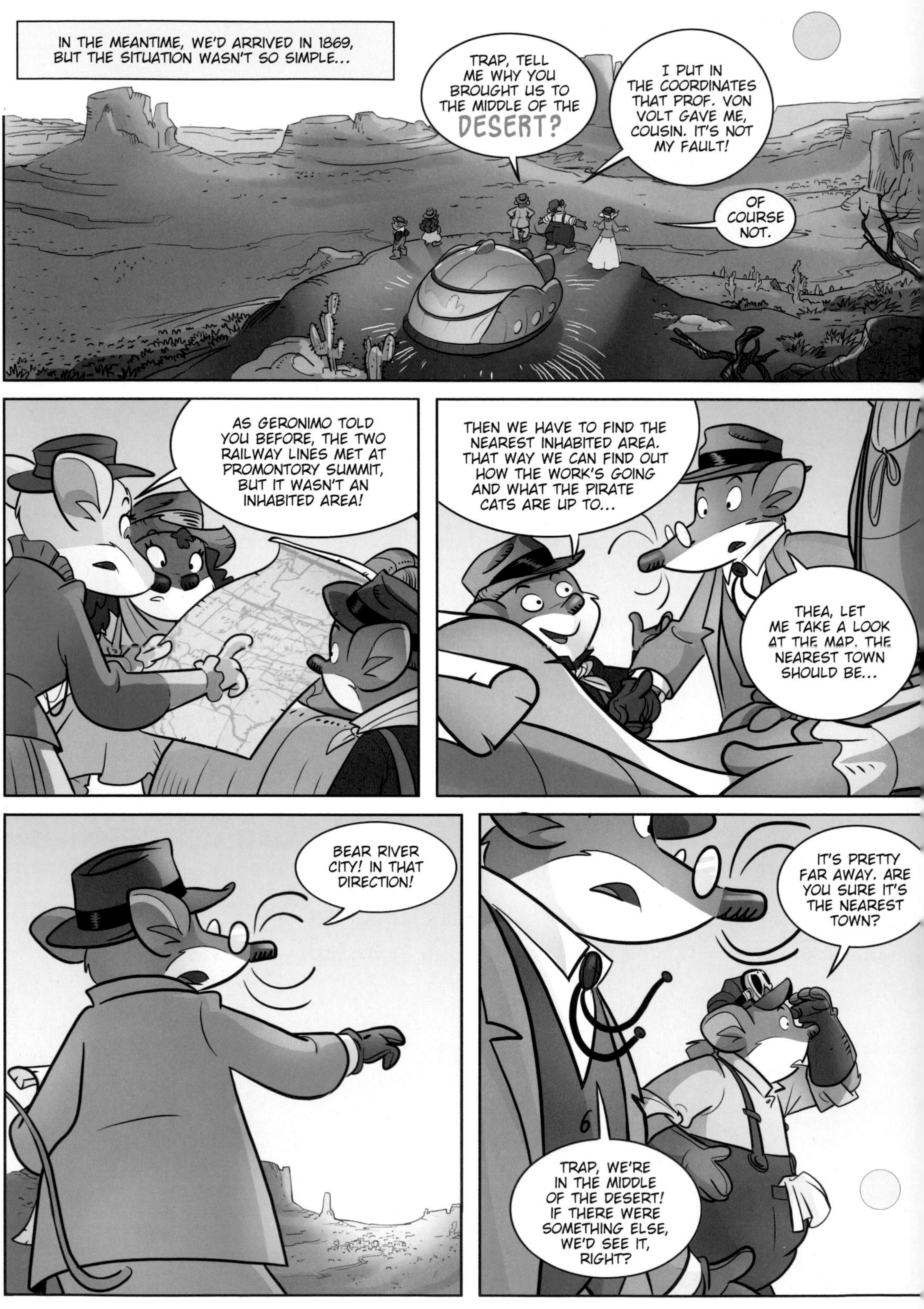
IN THE MEANTIME, WE'D ARRIVED IN 1869, BUT THE SITUATION WASN'T SO SIMPLE...
TRAP, TELL ME WHY YOU BROUGHT US TO THE MIDDLE OF THE DESERT?
I PUT IN THE COORDINATES THAT PROF. VON VOLT GAVE ME, COUSIN. IT'S NOT MY FAULT!
OF COURSE NOT.
AS GERONIMO TOLD YOU BEFORE, THE TWO RAILWAY LINES MET AT PROMONTORY SUMMIT, BUT IT WASN'T AN INHABITED AREA!
THEN WE HAVE TO FIND THE NEAREST INHABITED AREA. THAT WAY WE CAN FIND OUT HOW THE WORK'S GOING AND WHAT THE PIRATE CATS ARE UP TO...
THEA, LET ME TAKE A LOOK AT THE MAP. THE NEAREST TOWN SHOULD BE...
BEAR RIVER CITY! IN THAT DIRECTION!
IT'S PRETTY FAR AWAY. ARE YOU SURE IT'S THE NEAREST TOWN?
TRAP, WE'RE IN THE MIDDLE OF THE DESERT! IF THERE WERE SOMETHING ELSE, WE'D SEE IT, RIGHT?

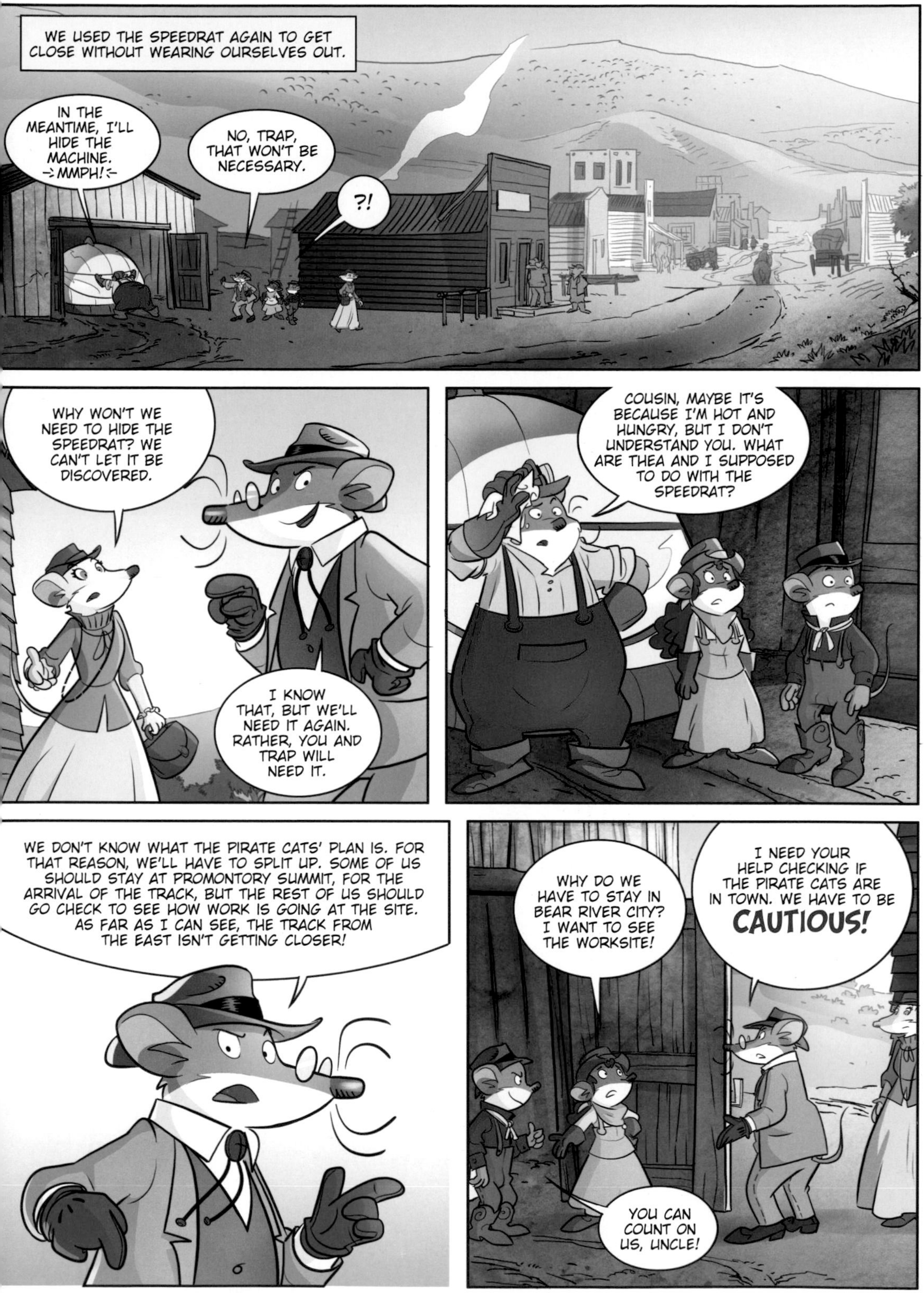
WE USED THE SPEEDRAT AGAIN TO GET CLOSE WITHOUT WEARING OURSELVES OUT.
IN THE MEANTIME, I'LL HIDE THE MACHINE. MMPH!
NO, TRAP, THAT WON'T BE NECESSARY.
?!
WHY WON'T WE NEED TO HIDE THE SPEEDRAT? WE CAN'T LET IT BE DISCOVERED.
I KNOW THAT, BUT WE'LL NEED IT AGAIN. RATHER, YOU AND TRAP WILL NEED IT.
COUSIN, MAYBE IT'S BECAUSE I'M HOT AND HUNGRY, BUT I DON'T UNDERSTAND YOU. WHAT ARE THEA AND I SUPPOSED TO DO WITH THE SPEEDRAT?
WE DON'T KNOW WHAT THE PIRATE CATS' PLAN IS. FOR THAT REASON, WE'LL HAVE TO SPLIT UP. SOME OF US SHOULD STAY AT PROMONTORY SUMMIT, FOR THE ARRIVAL OF THE TRACK, BUT THE REST OF US SHOULD GO CHECK TO SEE HOW WORK IS GOING AT THE SITE. AS FAR AS I CAN SEE, THE TRACK FROM THE EAST ISN'T GETTING CLOSER!
WHY DO WE HAVE TO STAY IN BEAR RIVER CITY? I WANT TO SEE THE WORKSITE!
I NEED YOUR HELP CHECKING IF THE PIRATE CATS ARE IN TOWN. WE HAVE TO BE CAUTIOUS!
YOU CAN COUNT ON US, UNCLE!

AND BESIDES, I'M VERY GLAD TO AVOID ANOTHER FLIGHT IN THE SPEEDRAT WITH TRAP! THAT WOULD BE THE THIRD IN A SHORT TIME!

HEE! HEE! HEE!

TRAP, YOU SHOULD TRY TO GET HIRED AS A WORKER AT THE CONSTRUCTION SITE. THEA, TRY TO KEEP OUR COUSIN FROM SLOWING DOWN THE CONSTRUCTION WORK.

HEY!

!

REMEMBER, WE DON'T KNOW WHERE OR WHEN THE PIRATE CATS WILL SWING INTO ACTION!

CALM DOWN, COUSIN, WE'LL SEE TO IT!

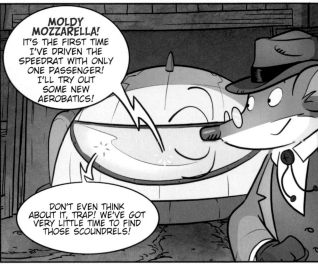

MOLDY MOZZARELLA! IT'S THE FIRST TIME I'VE DRIVEN THE SPEEDRAT WITH ONLY ONE PASSENGER! I'LL TRY OUT SOME NEW AEROBATICS!

DON'T EVEN THINK ABOUT IT, TRAP! WE'VE GOT VERY LITTLE TIME TO FIND THOSE SCOUNDRELS!

COME ON, KIDS, LET'S GO CHECK OUT THE WILD WEST!

THE WILD WEST (FAR WEST OR OLD WEST) WAS A TERM USED IN THE 1800s FOR THE REGION BETWEEN THE GREAT PLAINS AND THE ROCKY MOUNTAINS, EXTENDING WESTWARDS FROM THE MISSISSIPPI RIVER TO THE PACIFIC OCEAN AND TOWARDS CANADA. THE AREA WAS INHABITED BY NATIVE AMERICANS, THAT IS TO SAY, AMERICAN INDIANS.

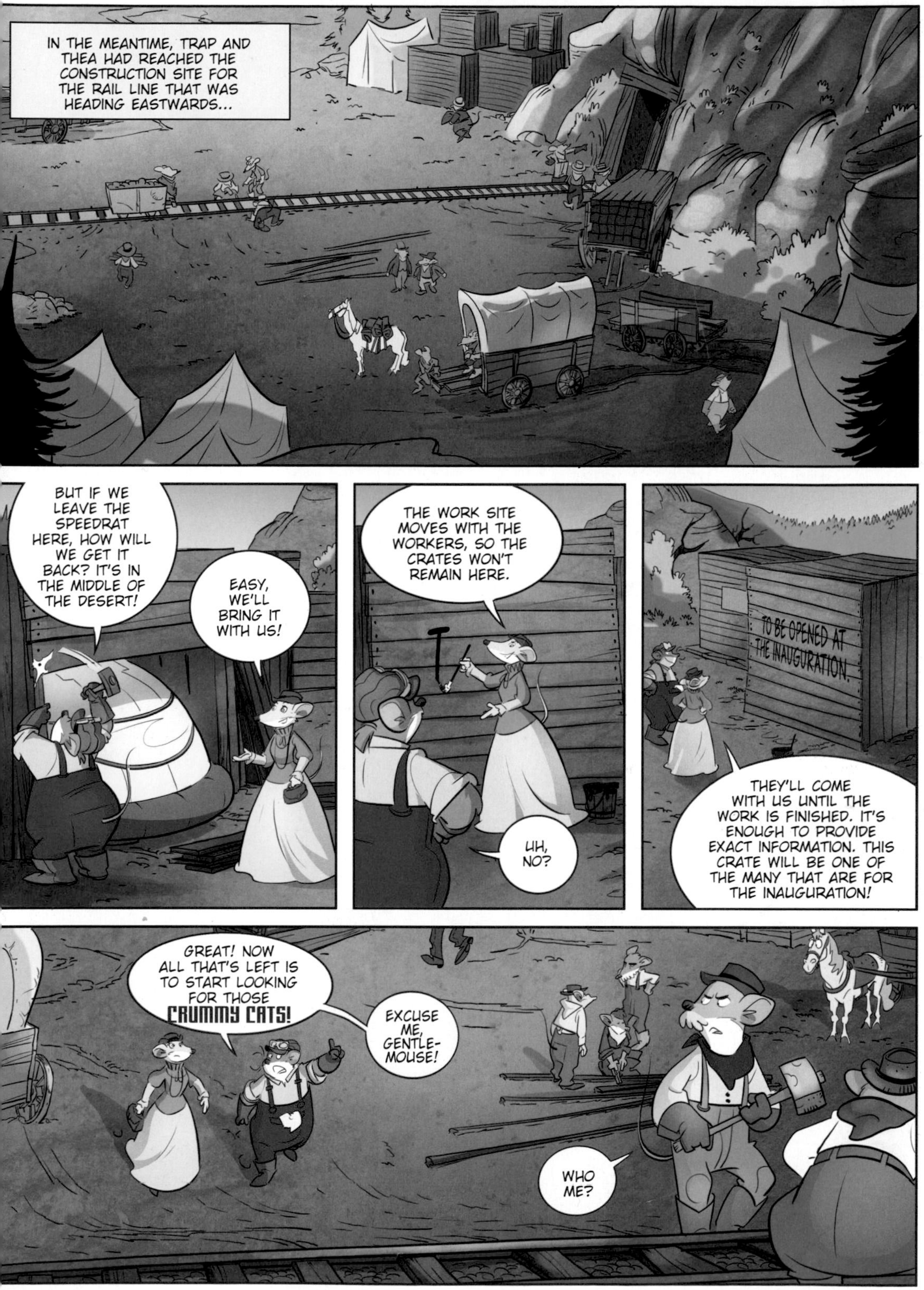
IN THE MEANTIME, TRAP AND THEA HAD REACHED THE CONSTRUCTION SITE FOR THE RAIL LINE THAT WAS HEADING EASTWARDS...
BUT IF WE LEAVE THE SPEEDRAT HERE, HOW WILL WE GET IT BACK? IT'S IN THE MIDDLE OF THE DESERT!
EASY, WE'LL BRING IT WITH US!
THE WORK SITE MOVES WITH THE WORKERS, SO THE CRATES WON'T REMAIN HERE.
UH, NO?
TO BE OPENED AT THE INAUGURATION.
THEY'LL COME WITH US UNTIL THE WORK IS FINISHED. IT'S ENOUGH TO PROVIDE EXACT INFORMATION. THIS CRATE WILL BE ONE OF THE MANY THAT ARE FOR THE INAUGURATION!
GREAT! NOW ALL THAT'S LEFT IS TO START LOOKING FOR THOSE CRUMMY CATS!
EXCUSE ME, GENTLE-MOUSE!
WHO ME?

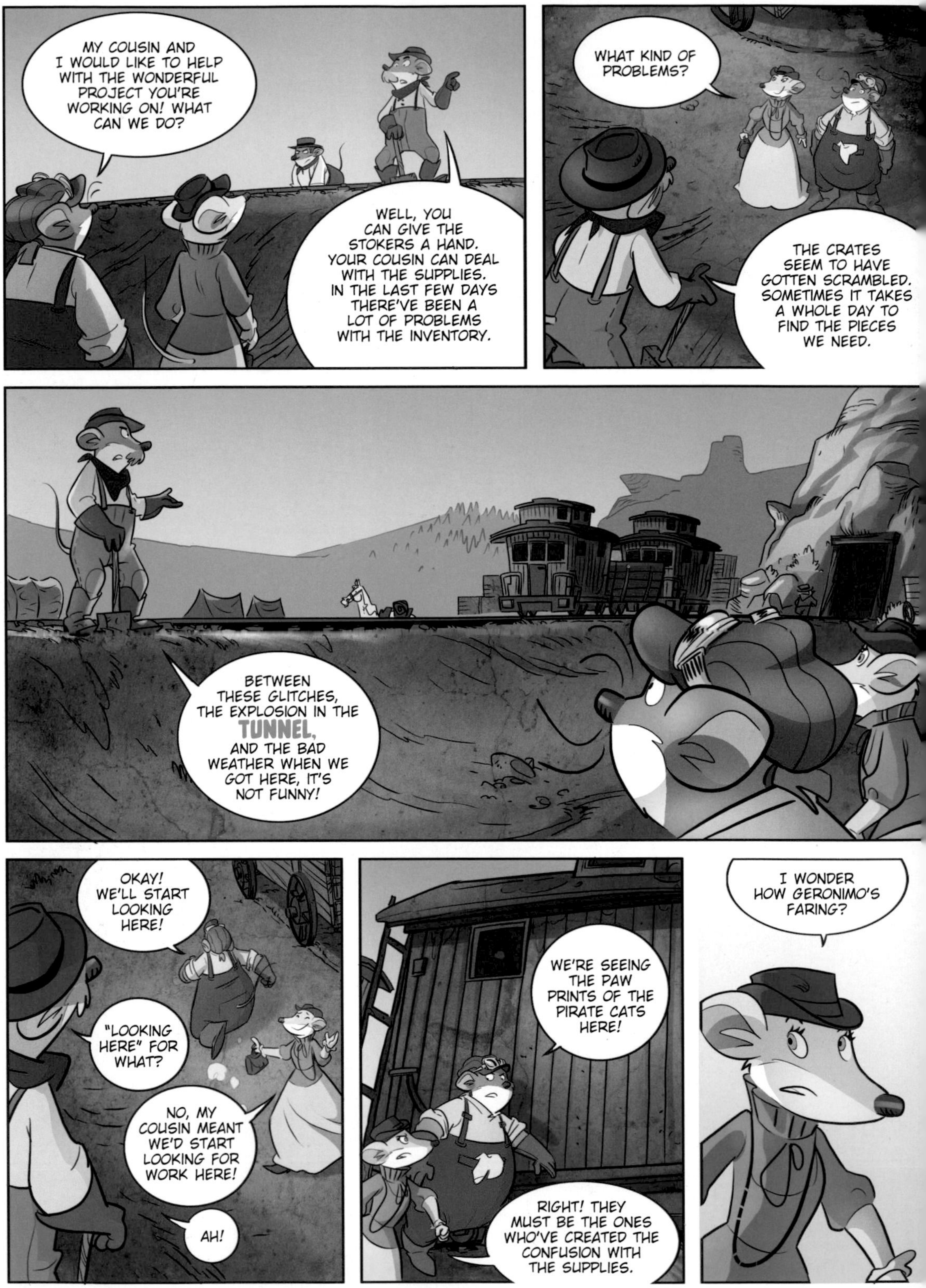
MY COUSIN AND I WOULD LIKE TO HELP WITH THE WONDERFUL PROJECT YOU'RE WORKING ON! WHAT CAN WE DO?
WELL, YOU CAN GIVE THE STOKERS A HAND. YOUR COUSIN CAN DEAL WITH THE SUPPLIES. IN THE LAST FEW DAYS THERE'VE BEEN A LOT OF PROBLEMS WITH THE INVENTORY.
WHAT KIND OF PROBLEMS?
THE CRATES SEEM TO HAVE GOTTEN SCRAMBLED. SOMETIMES IT TAKES A WHOLE DAY TO FIND THE PIECES WE NEED.
BETWEEN THESE GLITCHES, THE EXPLOSION IN THE TUNNEL, AND THE BAD WEATHER WHEN WE GOT HERE, IT'S NOT FUNNY!
OKAY! WE'LL START LOOKING HERE!
"LOOKING HERE" FOR WHAT?
NO, MY COUSIN MEANT WE'D START LOOKING FOR WORK HERE!
AH!
WE'RE SEEING THE PAW PRINTS OF THE PIRATE CATS HERE!
RIGHT! THEY MUST BE THE ONES WHO'VE CREATED THE CONFUSION WITH THE SUPPLIES.
I WONDER HOW GERONIMO'S FARING?

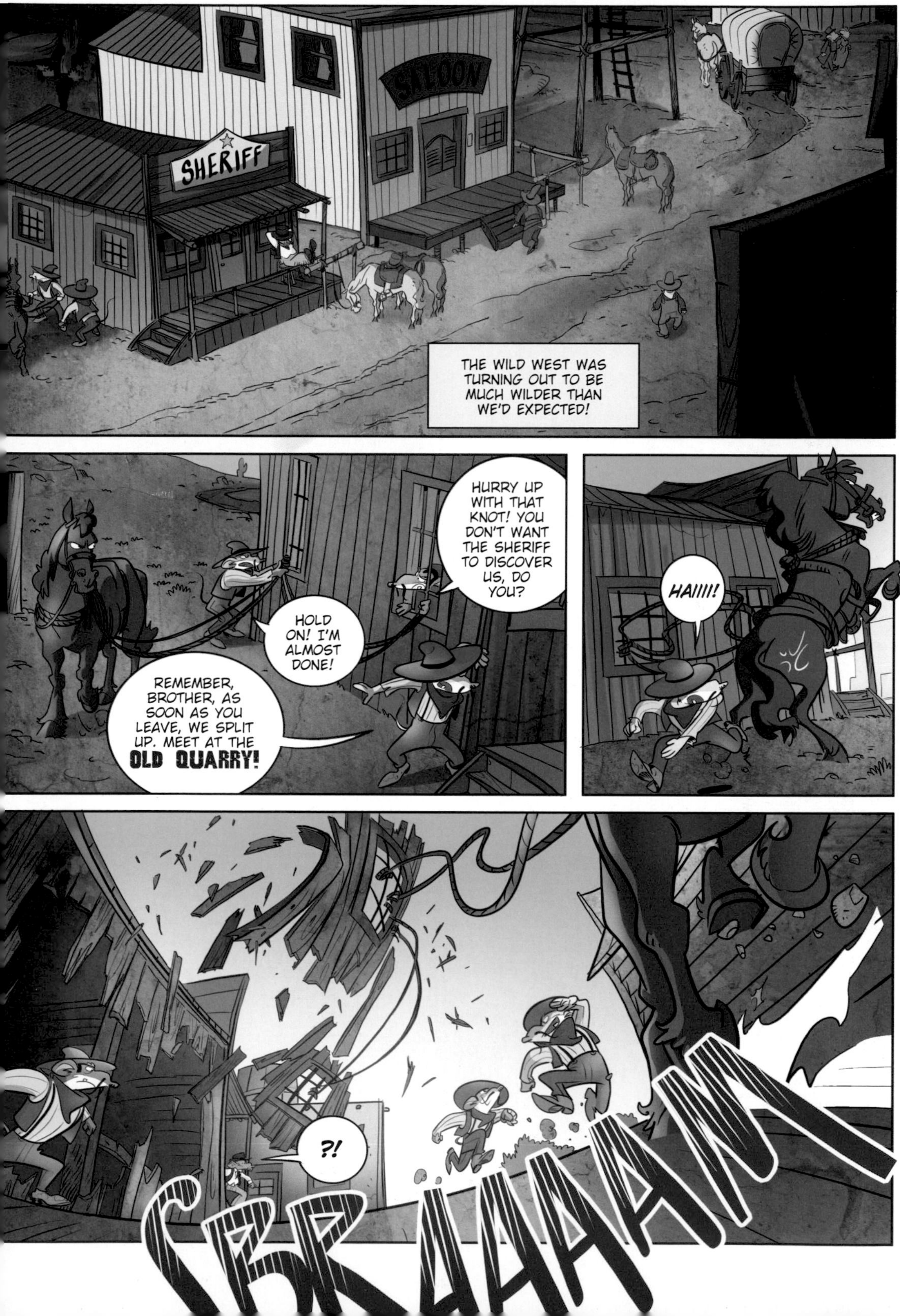

SHERIFF
SALOON
THE WILD WEST WAS TURNING OUT TO BE MUCH WILDER THAN WE'D EXPECTED!
HURRY UP WITH THAT KNOT! YOU DON'T WANT THE SHERIFF TO DISCOVER US, DO YOU?
HOLD ON! I'M ALMOST DONE!
REMEMBER, BROTHER, AS SOON AS YOU LEAVE, WE SPLIT UP. MEET AT THE OLD QUARRY!
HAIIII!
?!
CRRAAAAM

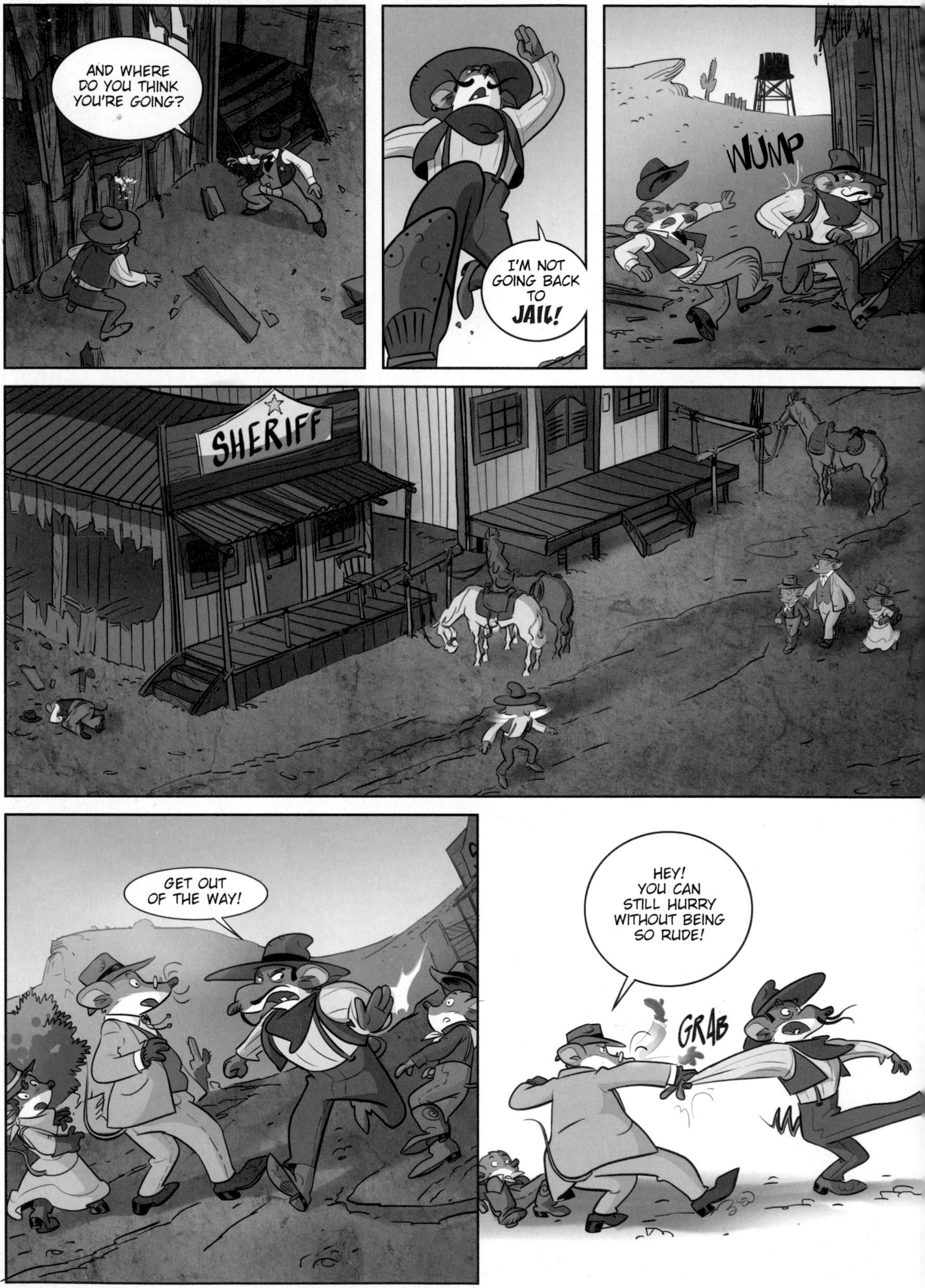
AND WHERE DO YOU THINK YOU'RE GOING?
I'M NOT GOING BACK TO JAIL!
WUMP
SHERIFF
GET OUT OF THE WAY!
HEY! YOU CAN STILL HURRY WITHOUT BEING SO RUDE!
GRAB

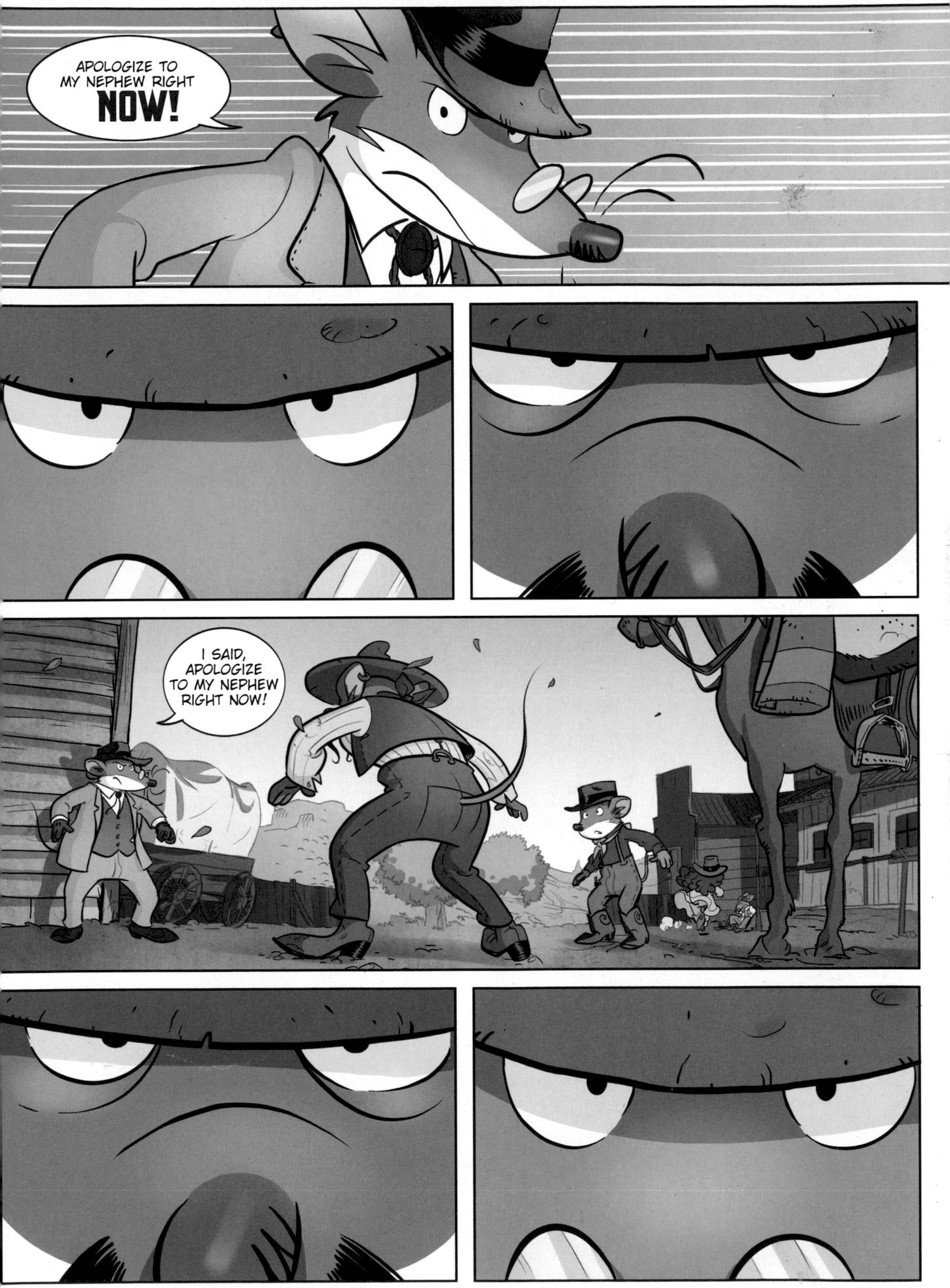
APOLOGIZE TO MY NEPHEW RIGHT NOW!
I SAID, APOLOGIZE TO MY NEPHEW RIGHT NOW!

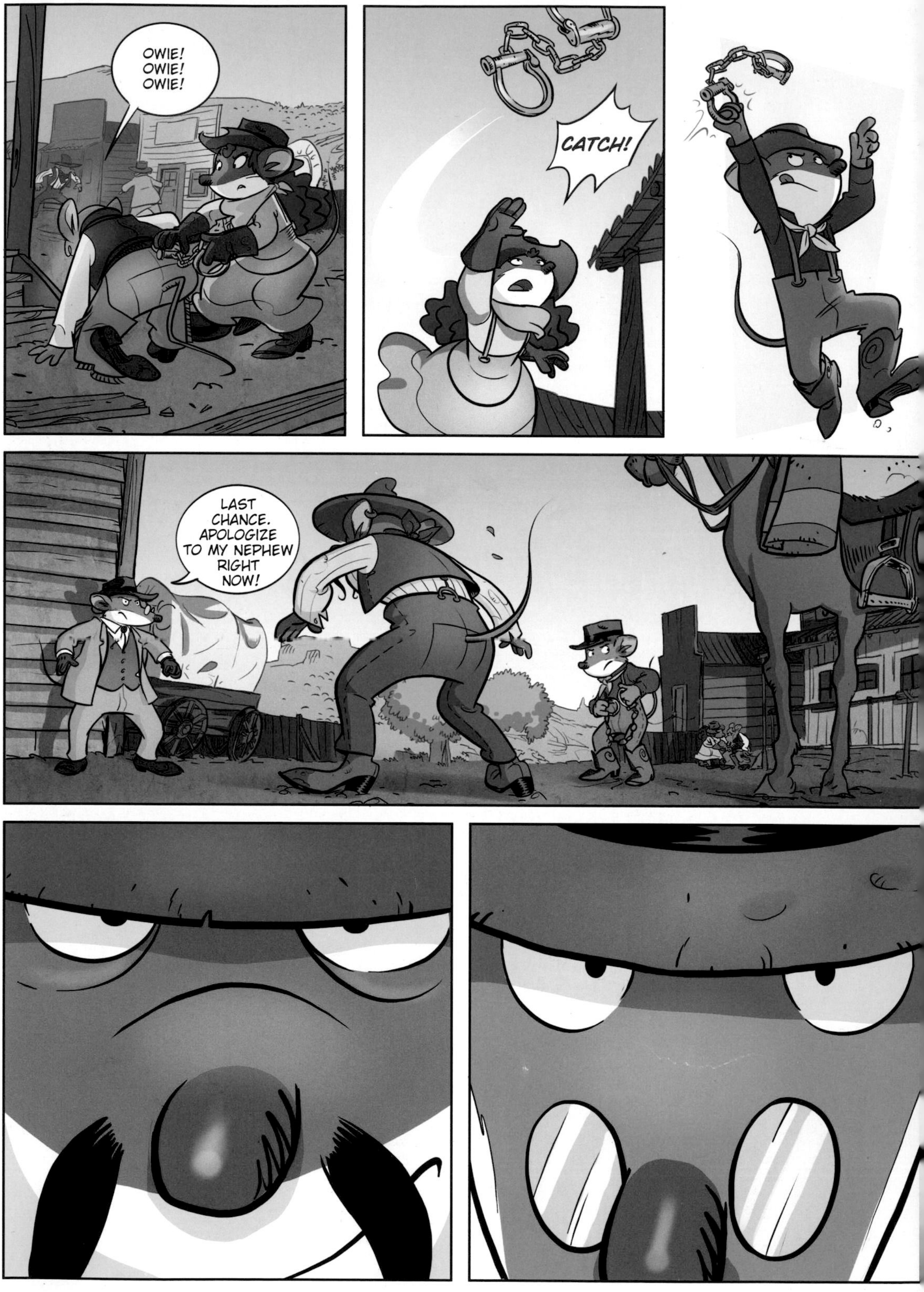
OWIE! OWIE! OWIE!
CATCH!
LAST CHANCE. APOLOGIZE TO MY NEPHEW RIGHT NOW!

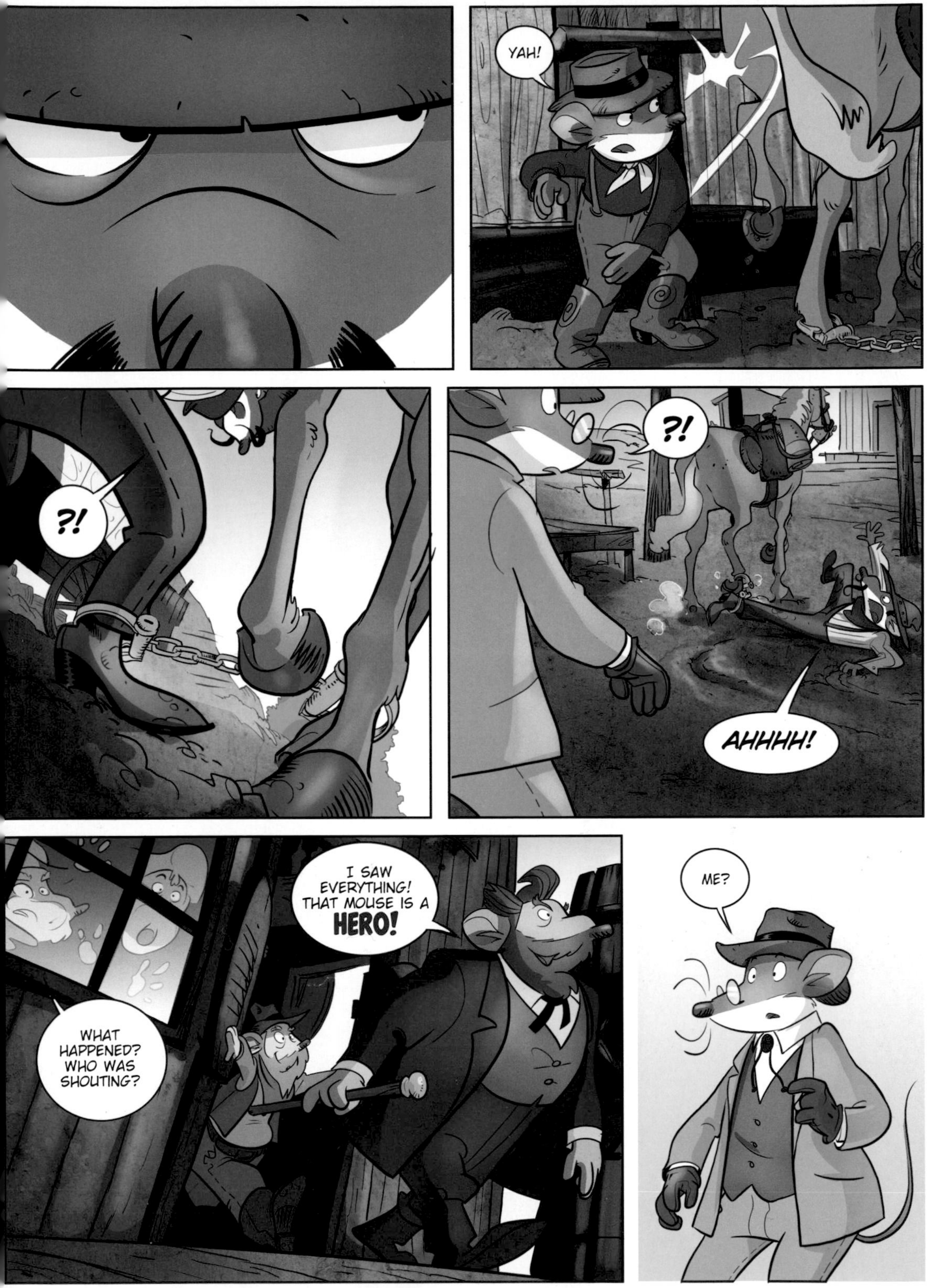
YAH!
?!
?!
AHHHH!
WHAT HAPPENED? WHO WAS SHOUTING?
I SAW EVERYTHING! THAT MOUSE IS A HERO!
ME?

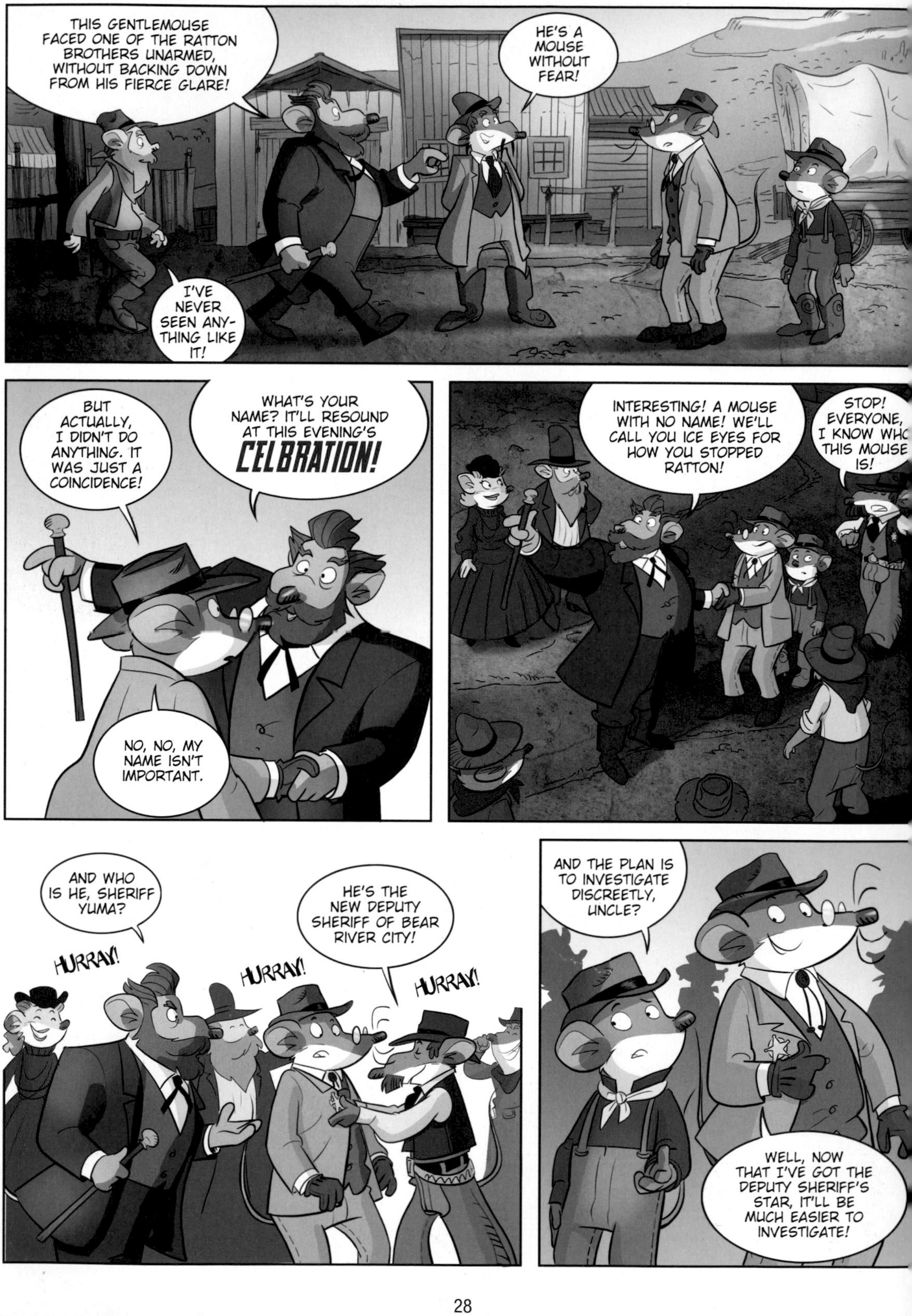

THIS GENTLEMOUSE FACED ONE OF THE RATTON BROTHERS UNARMED, WITHOUT BACKING DOWN FROM HIS FIERCE GLARE!
I'VE NEVER SEEN ANY-THING LIKE IT!
HE'S A MOUSE WITHOUT FEAR!
BUT ACTUALLY, I DIDN'T DO ANYTHING. IT WAS JUST A COINCIDENCE!
WHAT'S YOUR NAME? IT'LL RESOUND AT THIS EVENING'S CELBRATION!
NO, NO, MY NAME ISN'T IMPORTANT.
INTERESTING! A MOUSE WITH NO NAME! WE'LL CALL YOU ICE EYES FOR HOW YOU STOPPED RATTON!
STOP! EVERYONE, I KNOW WHO THIS MOUSE IS!
AND WHO IS HE, SHERIFF YUMA?
HE'S THE NEW DEPUTY SHERIFF OF BEAR RIVER CITY!
HURRAY!
HURRAY!
HURRAY!
AND THE PLAN IS TO INVESTIGATE DISCREETLY, UNCLE?
WELL, NOW THAT I'VE GOT THE DEPUTY SHERIFF'S STAR, IT'LL BE MUCH EASIER TO INVESTIGATE!

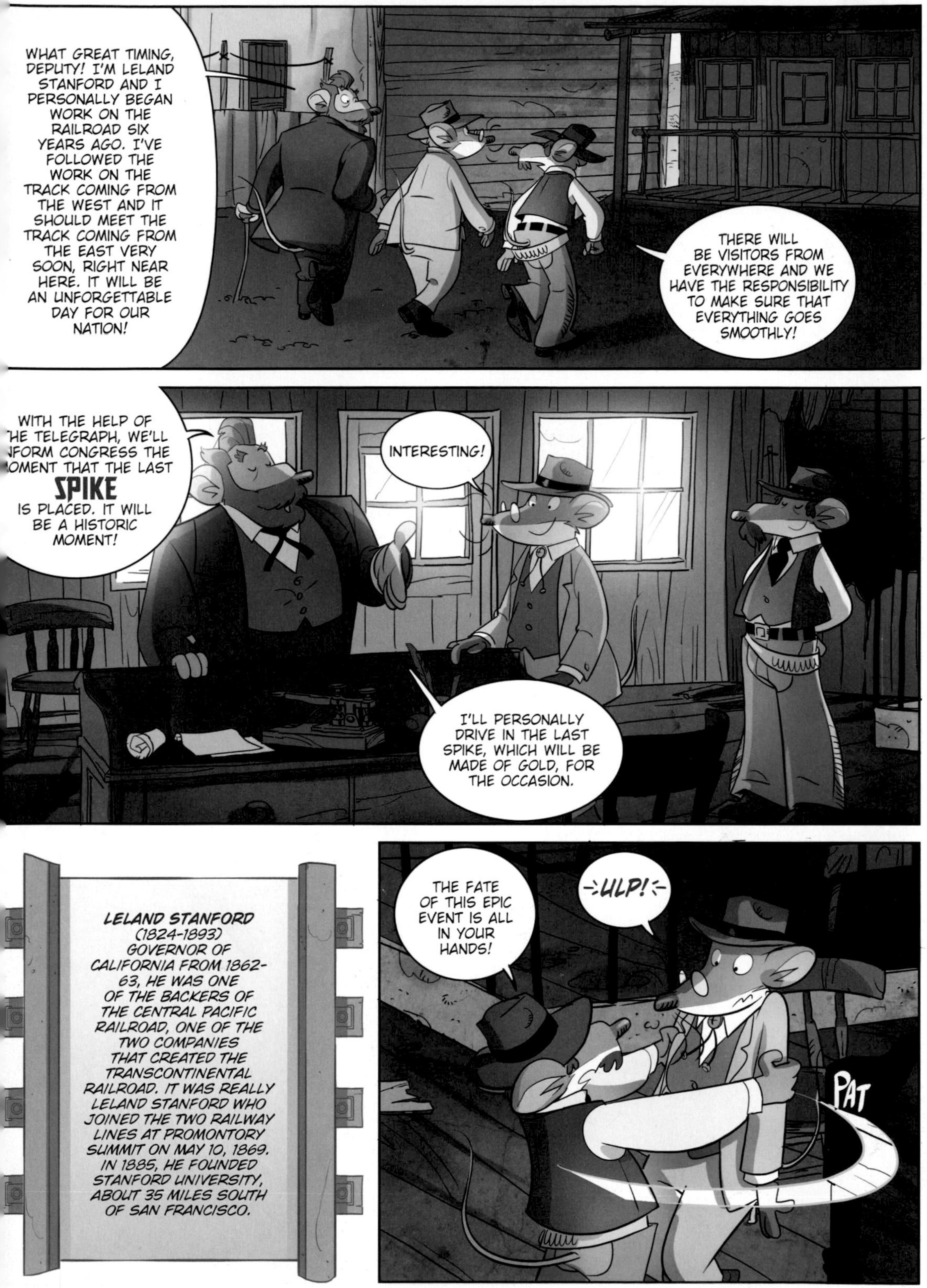
WHAT GREAT TIMING, DEPUTY! I'M LELAND STANFORD AND I PERSONALLY BEGAN WORK ON THE RAILROAD SIX YEARS AGO. I'VE FOLLOWED THE WORK ON THE TRACK COMING FROM THE WEST AND IT SHOULD MEET THE TRACK COMING FROM THE EAST VERY SOON, RIGHT NEAR HERE. IT WILL BE AN UNFORGETTABLE DAY FOR OUR NATION!
THERE WILL BE VISITORS FROM EVERYWHERE AND WE HAVE THE RESPONSIBILITY TO MAKE SURE THAT EVERYTHING GOES SMOOTHLY!
WITH THE HELP OF THE TELEGRAPH, WE'LL INFORM CONGRESS THE MOMENT THAT THE LAST SPIKE IS PLACED. IT WILL BE A HISTORIC MOMENT!
INTERESTING!
I'LL PERSONALLY DRIVE IN THE LAST SPIKE, WHICH WILL BE MADE OF GOLD, FOR THE OCCASION.
LELAND STANFORD (1824-1893) GOVERNOR OF CALIFORNIA FROM 1862-63, HE WAS ONE OF THE BACKERS OF THE CENTRAL PACIFIC RAILROAD, ONE OF THE TWO COMPANIES THAT CREATED THE TRANSCONTINENTAL RAILROAD. IT WAS REALLY LELAND STANFORD WHO JOINED THE TWO RAILWAY LINES AT PROMONTORY SUMMIT ON MAY 10, 1869. IN 1885, HE FOUNDED STANFORD UNIVERSITY, ABOUT 35 MILES SOUTH OF SAN FRANCISCO.
THE FATE OF THIS EPIC EVENT IS ALL IN YOUR HANDS!
ULP!
PAT

IN THE MEANTIME, THEA AND TRAP WERE ALSO VERY BUSY...

I CAN'T OPEN AND CLOSE CRATES ANY MORE!

ONE CRATE WAS ADDED TO THIS LIST AFTER WORK STARTED. IT MUST HAVE BEEN THE PIRATE CATS WHO MARKED IT ON THE LIST, TO HIDE THE CATJET.

BUT WE'VE OPENED ALMOST ALL OF THEM! AND NOW THE WORKERS ARE STARTING TO GET SUSPICIOUS OF US!

THAT'S EXACTLY WHY WE HAVE TO TAKE CARE OF THIS! THESE DAYS OF BAD WEATHER HAVE SLOWED THE WORK DOWN, BUT WE'RE EXPECTING TO GET TO PROMONTORY SUMMIT SOON.

UHM, THEA?

WHAT IS IT?

TO BE O AT INAU

THE CRATE THAT WAS ADDED TO THE LIST ISN'T OURS, RIGHT?

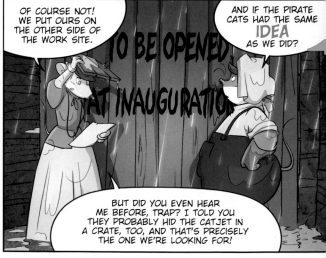

OF COURSE NOT! WE PUT OURS ON THE OTHER SIDE OF THE WORK SITE.

TO BE OPENED AT INAUGURATION

AND IF THE PIRATE CATS HAD THE SAME IDEA AS WE DID?

BUT DID YOU EVEN HEAR ME BEFORE, TRAP? I TOLD YOU THEY PROBABLY HID THE CATJET IN A CRATE, TOO, AND THAT'S PRECISELY THE ONE WE'RE LOOKING FOR!

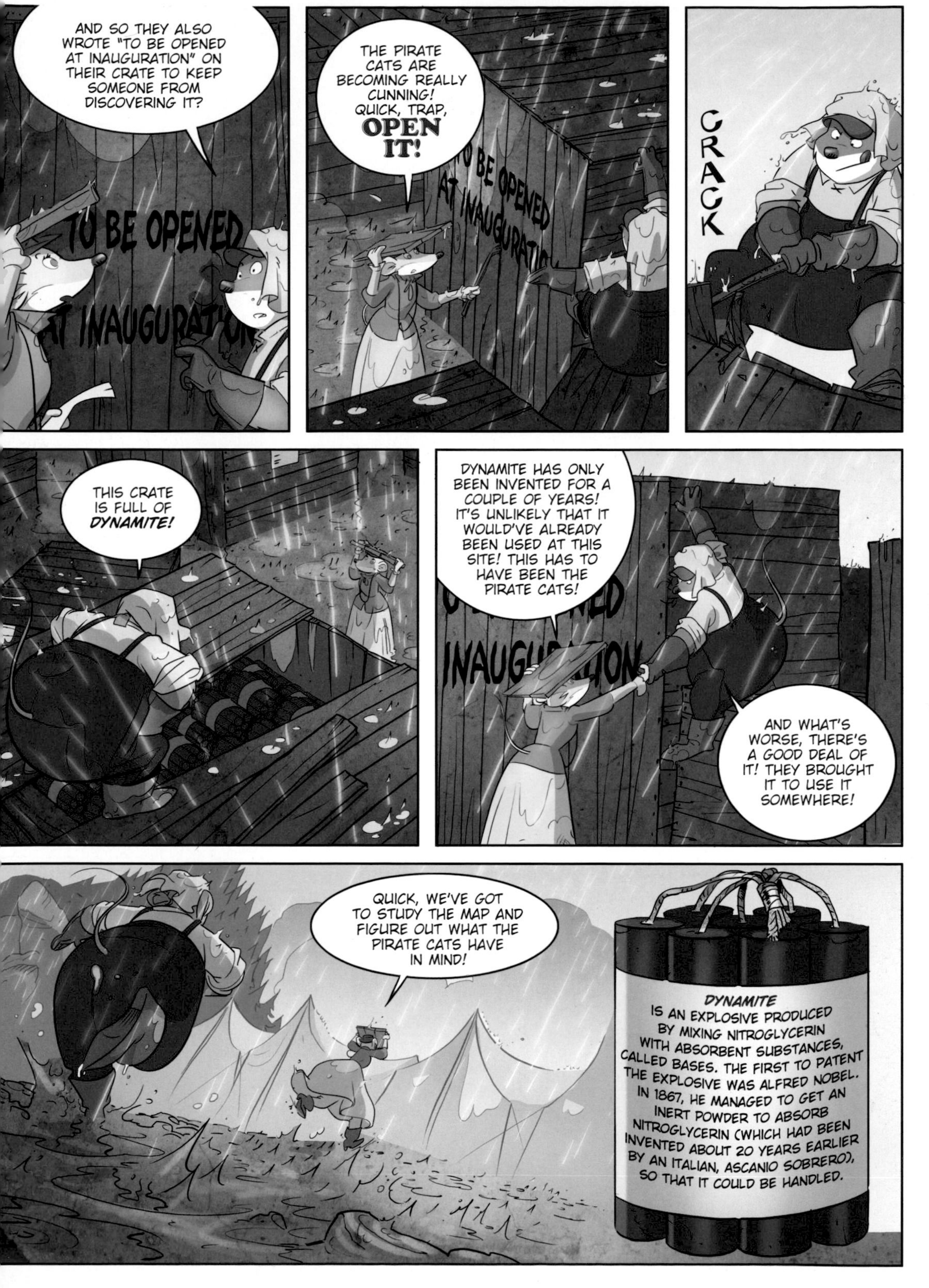
AND SO THEY ALSO WROTE "TO BE OPENED AT INAUGURATION" ON THEIR CRATE TO KEEP SOMEONE FROM DISCOVERING IT?
TO BE OPENED AT INAUGURATION
THE PIRATE CATS ARE BECOMING REALLY CUNNING! QUICK, TRAP, OPEN IT!
CRACK
THIS CRATE IS FULL OF DYNAMITE!
DYNAMITE HAS ONLY BEEN INVENTED FOR A COUPLE OF YEARS! IT'S UNLIKELY THAT IT WOULD'VE ALREADY BEEN USED AT THIS SITE! THIS HAS TO HAVE BEEN THE PIRATE CATS!
AND WHAT'S WORSE, THERE'S A GOOD DEAL OF IT! THEY BROUGHT IT TO USE IT SOMEWHERE!
QUICK, WE'VE GOT TO STUDY THE MAP AND FIGURE OUT WHAT THE PIRATE CATS HAVE IN MIND!
DYNAMITE
IS AN EXPLOSIVE PRODUCED BY MIXING NITROGLYCERIN WITH ABSORBENT SUBSTANCES, CALLED BASES. THE FIRST TO PATENT THE EXPLOSIVE WAS ALFRED NOBEL. IN 1867, HE MANAGED TO GET AN INERT POWDER TO ABSORB NITROGLYCERIN (WHICH HAD BEEN INVENTED ABOUT 20 YEARS EARLIER BY AN ITALIAN, ASCANIO SOBRERO), SO THAT IT COULD BE HANDLED.

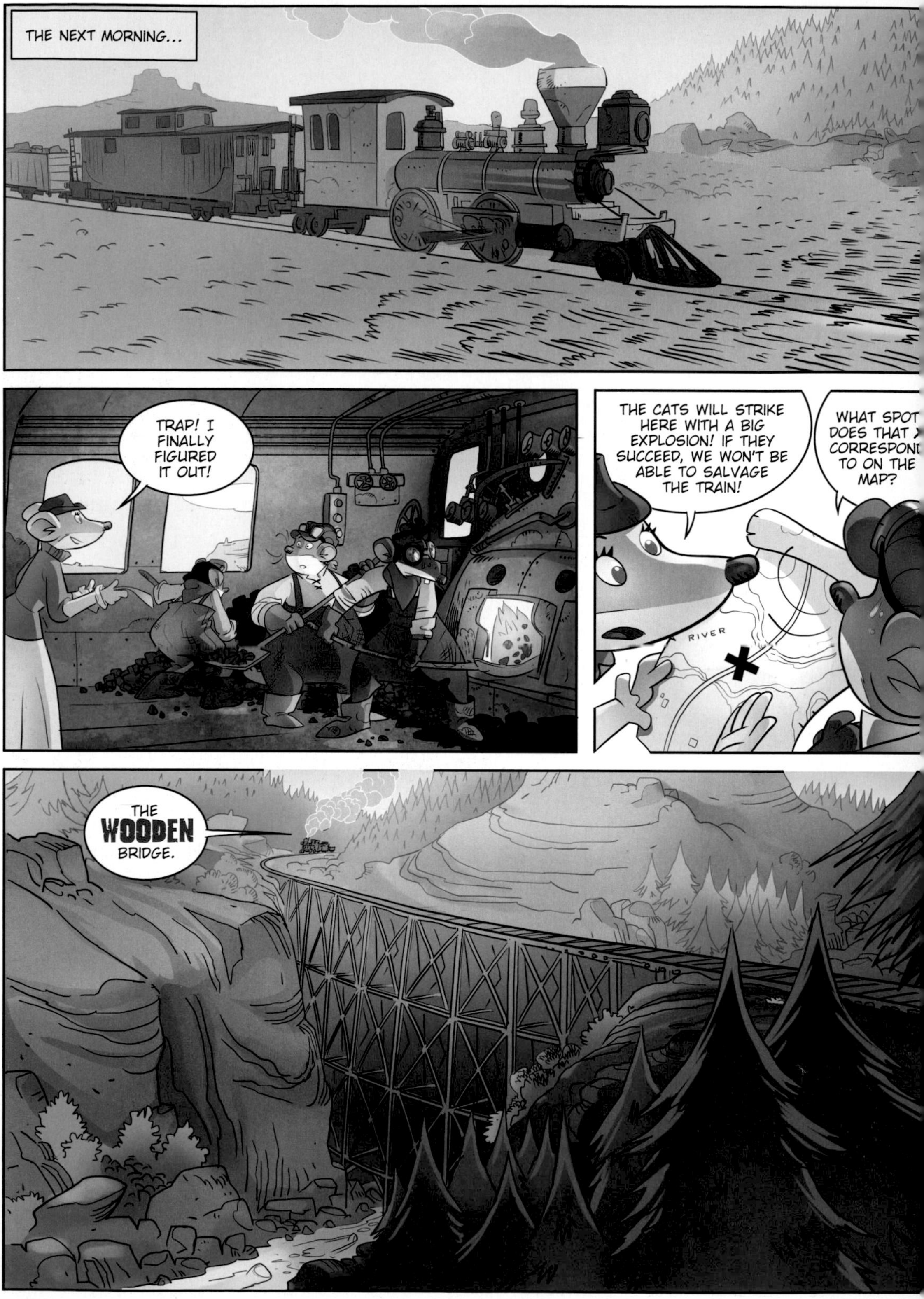
THE NEXT MORNING...
TRAP! I FINALLY FIGURED IT OUT!
THE CATS WILL STRIKE HERE WITH A BIG EXPLOSION! IF THEY SUCCEED, WE WON'T BE ABLE TO SALVAGE THE TRAIN!
WHAT SPOT DOES THAT X CORRESPOND TO ON THE MAP?
RIVER
THE WOODEN BRIDGE.

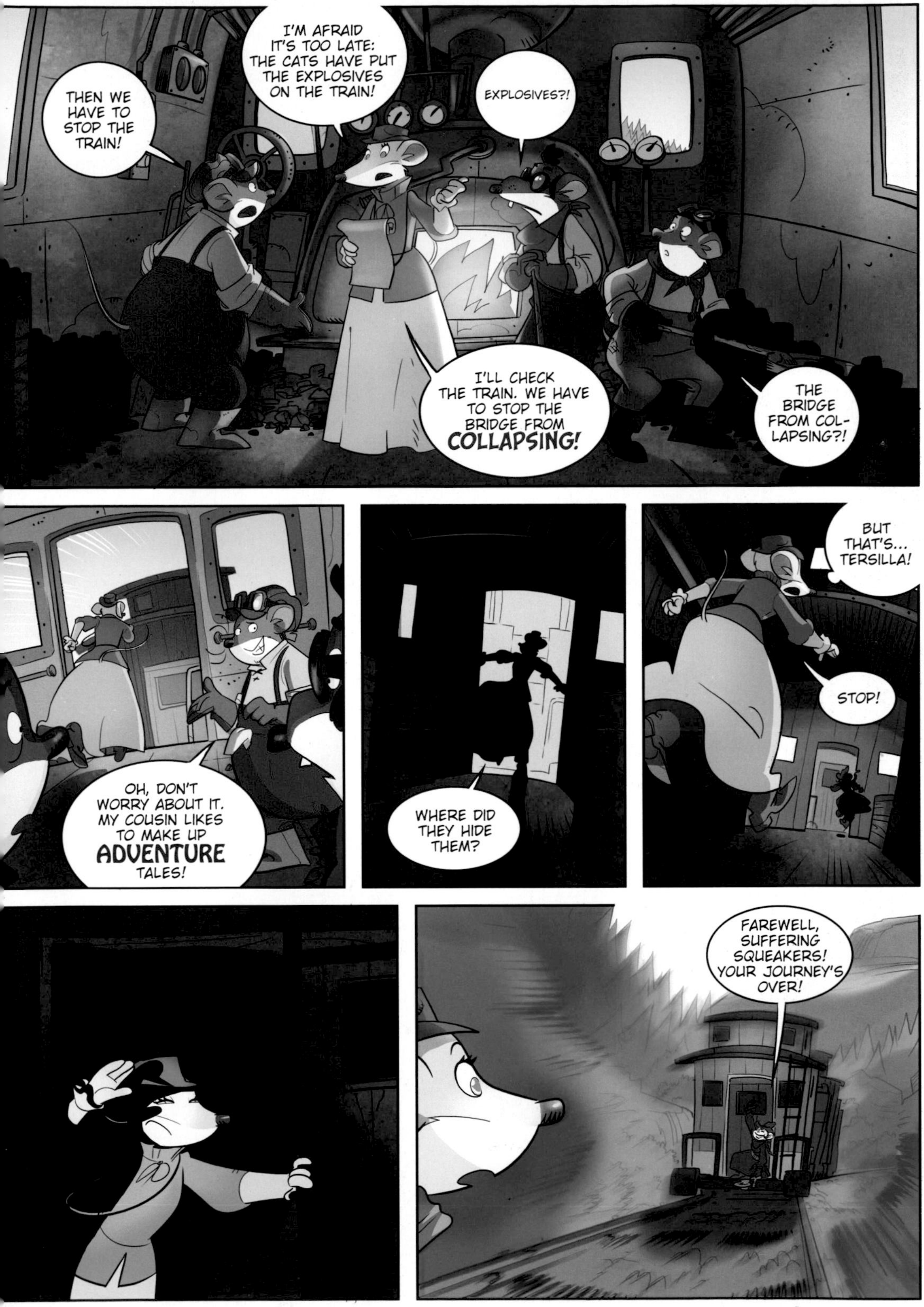
THEN WE HAVE TO STOP THE TRAIN!
I'M AFRAID IT'S TOO LATE: THE CATS HAVE PUT THE EXPLOSIVES ON THE TRAIN!
EXPLOSIVES?!
I'LL CHECK THE TRAIN. WE HAVE TO STOP THE BRIDGE FROM COLLAPSING!
THE BRIDGE FROM COL-LAPSING?!
OH, DON'T WORRY ABOUT IT. MY COUSIN LIKES TO MAKE UP ADVENTURE TALES!
WHERE DID THEY HIDE THEM?
BUT THAT'S... TERSILLA!
STOP!
FAREWELL, SUFFERING SQUEAKERS! YOUR JOURNEY'S OVER!

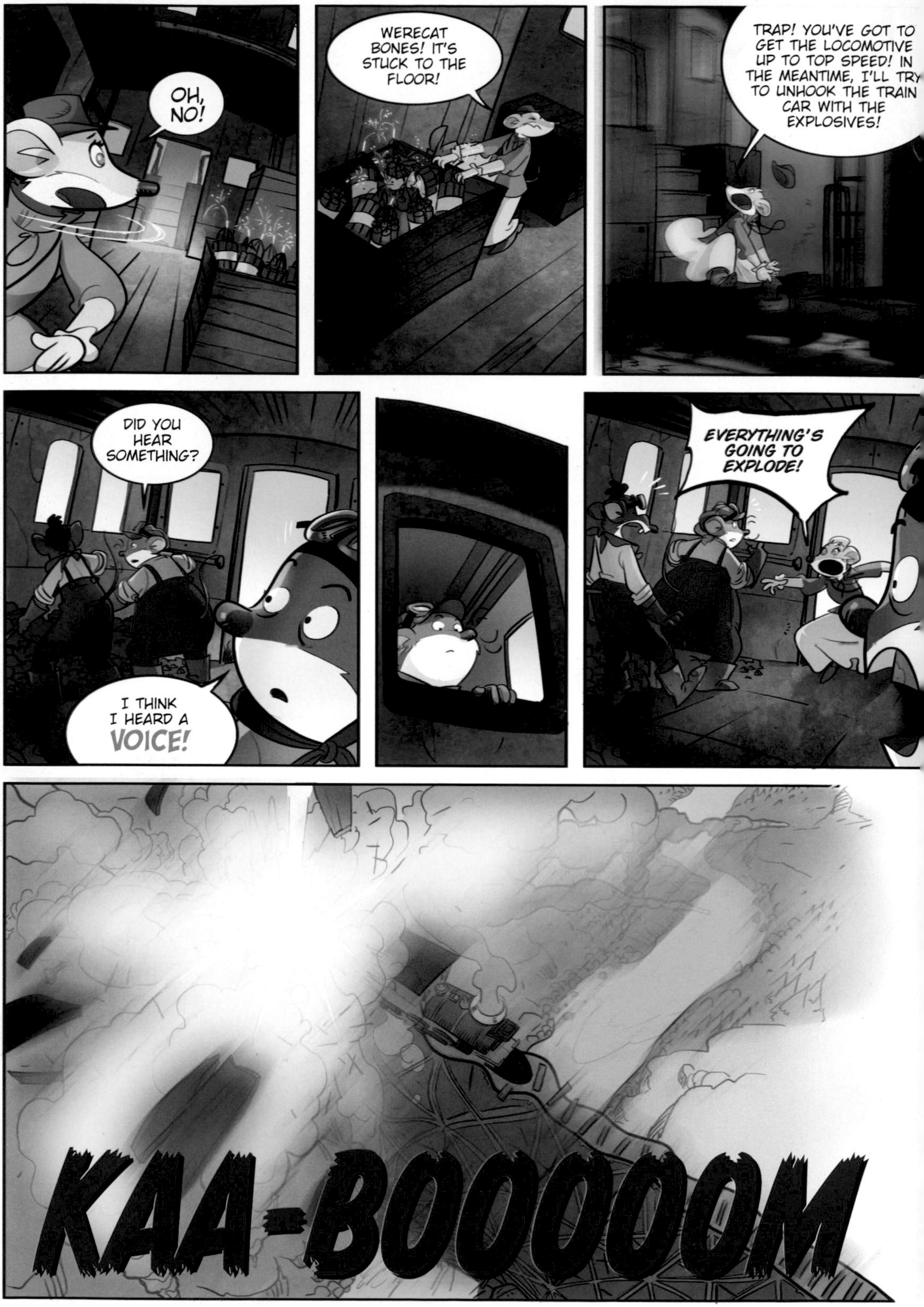
OH, NO!
WERECAT BONES! IT'S STUCK TO THE FLOOR!
TRAP! YOU'VE GOT TO GET THE LOCOMOTIVE UP TO TOP SPEED! IN THE MEANTIME, I'LL TRY TO UNHOOK THE TRAIN CAR WITH THE EXPLOSIVES!
DID YOU HEAR SOMETHING?
I THINK I HEARD A VOICE!
EVERYTHING'S GOING TO EXPLODE!
KAA-BOOOOOOM

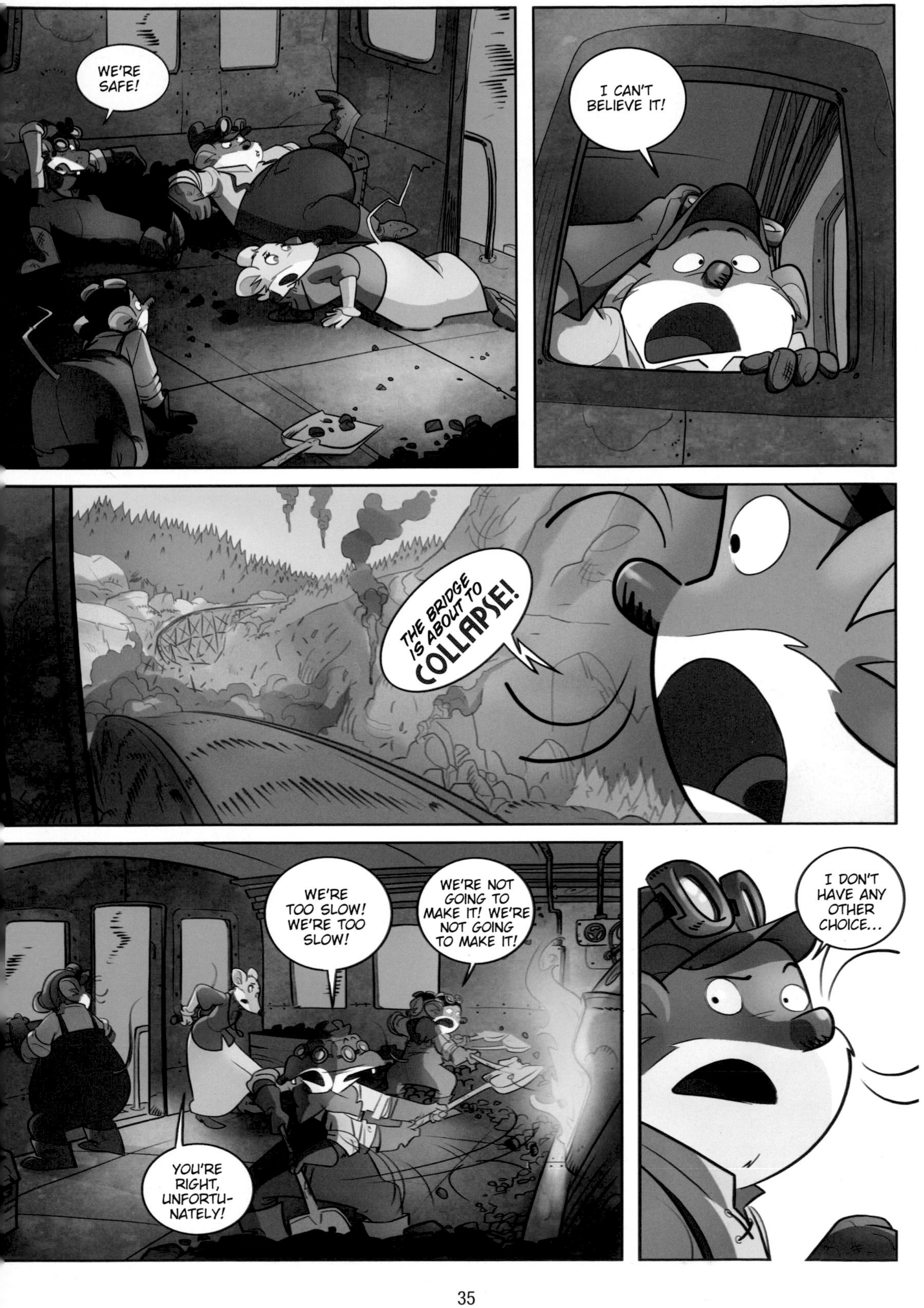
WE'RE SAFE!
I CAN'T BELIEVE IT!
THE BRIDGE IS ABOUT TO COLLAPSE!
WE'RE TOO SLOW! WE'RE TOO SLOW!
WE'RE NOT GOING TO MAKE IT! WE'RE NOT GOING TO MAKE IT!
YOU'RE RIGHT, UNFORTU-NATELY!
I DON'T HAVE ANY OTHER CHOICE...

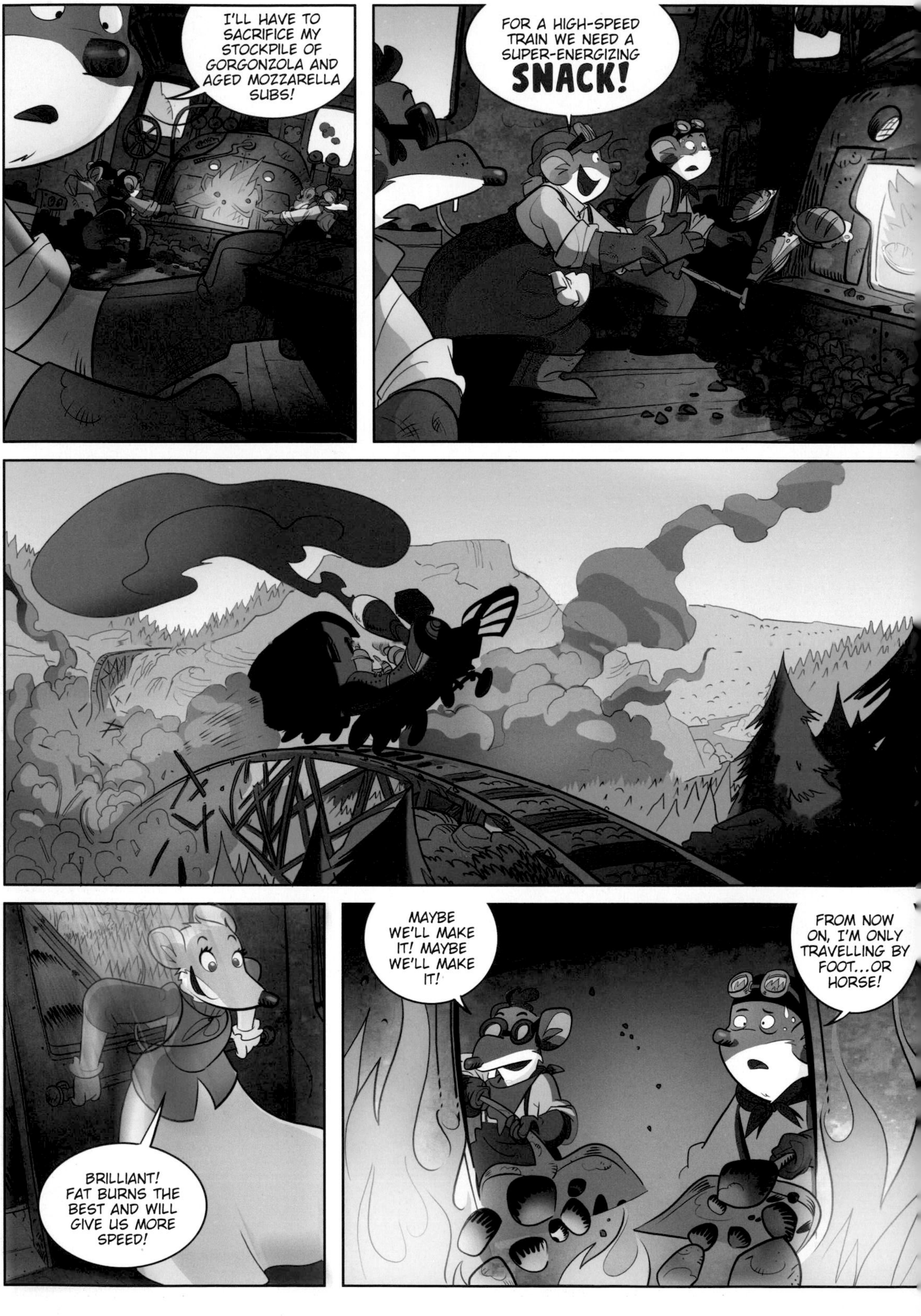
I'LL HAVE TO SACRIFICE MY STOCKPILE OF GORGONZOLA AND AGED MOZZARELLA SUBS!
FOR A HIGH-SPEED TRAIN WE NEED A SUPER-ENERGIZING SNACK!
BRILLIANT! FAT BURNS THE BEST AND WILL GIVE US MORE SPEED!
MAYBE WE'LL MAKE IT! MAYBE WE'LL MAKE IT!
FROM NOW ON, I'M ONLY TRAVELLING BY FOOT...OR HORSE!

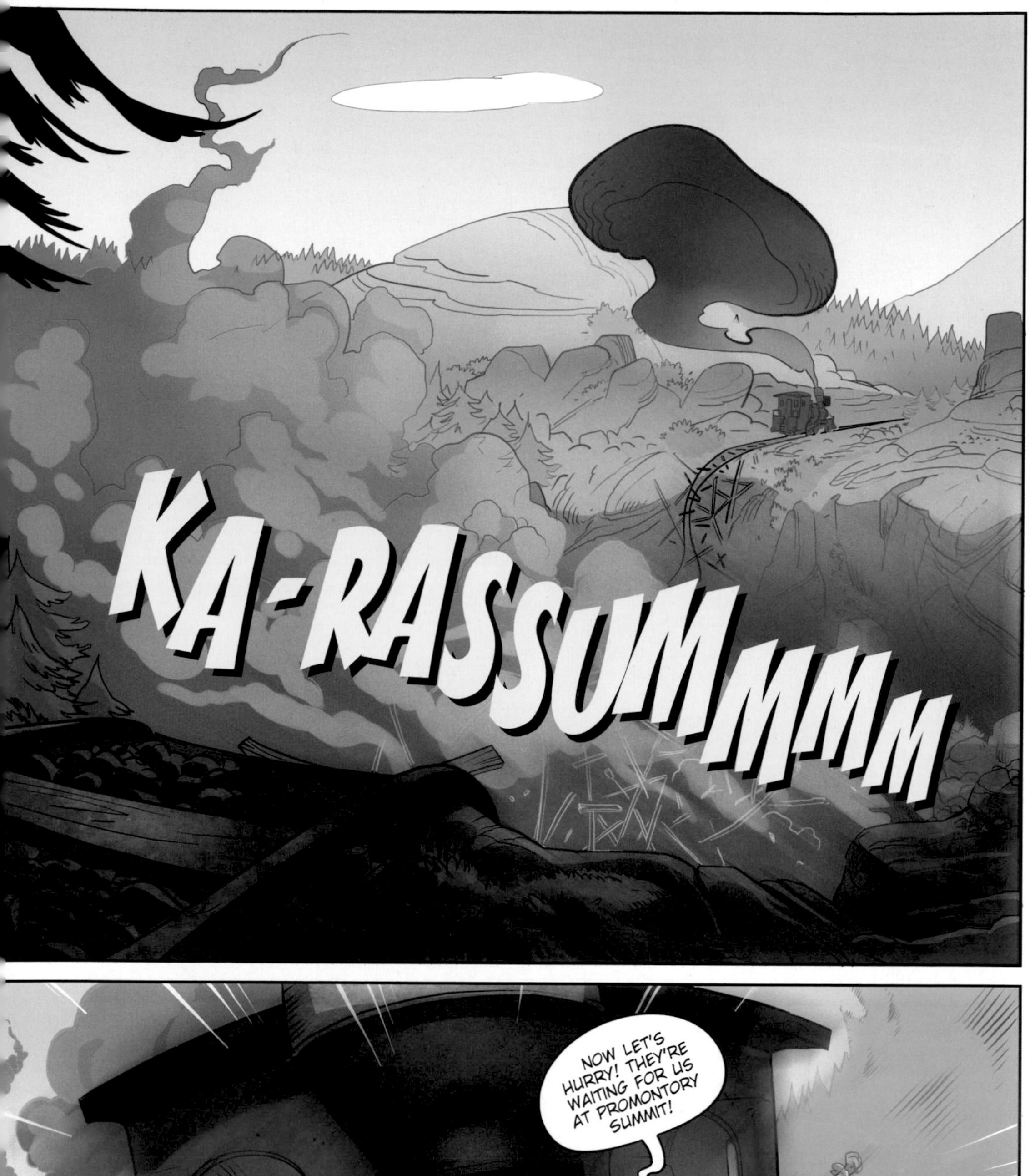
KA-RASSUMMMM

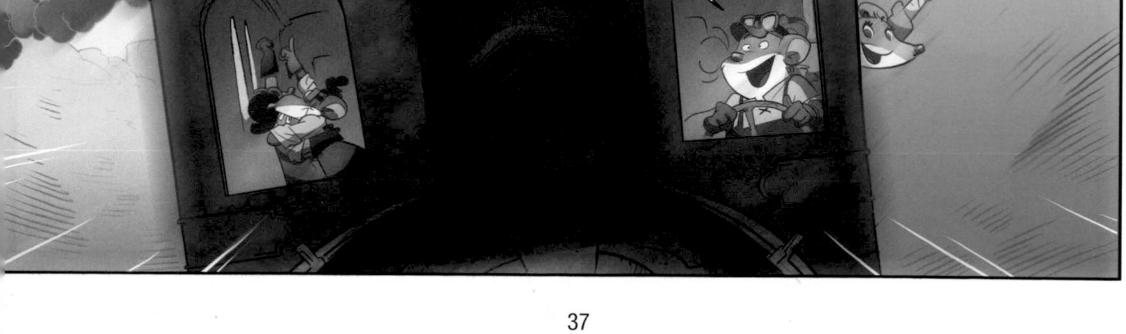
NOW LET'S HURRY! THEY'RE WAITING FOR US AT PROMONTORY SUMMIT!

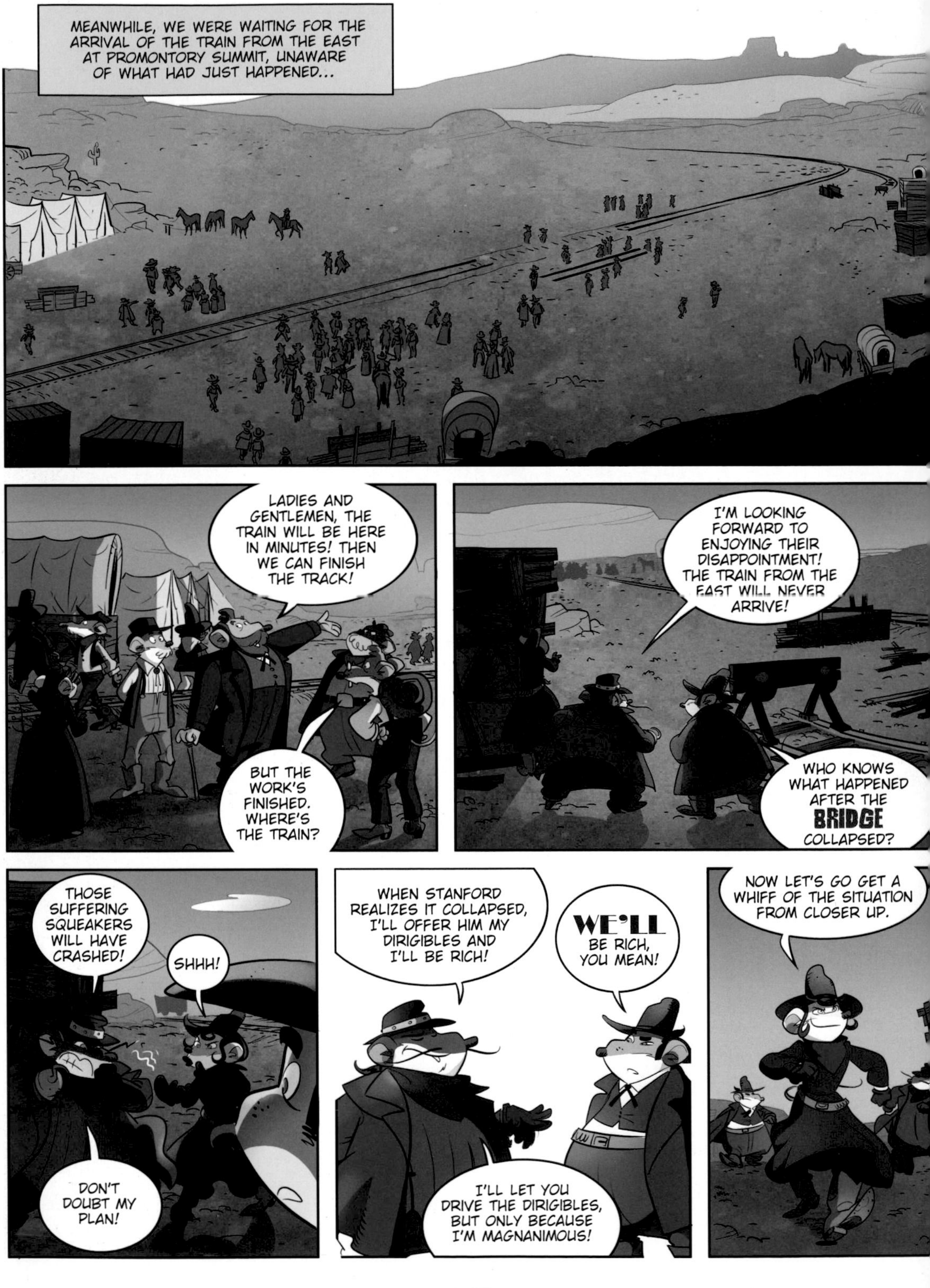

MEANWHILE, WE WERE WAITING FOR THE ARRIVAL OF THE TRAIN FROM THE EAST AT PROMONTORY SUMMIT, UNAWARE OF WHAT HAD JUST HAPPENED...
LADIES AND GENTLEMEN, THE TRAIN WILL BE HERE IN MINUTES! THEN WE CAN FINISH THE TRACK!
BUT THE WORK'S FINISHED. WHERE'S THE TRAIN?
I'M LOOKING FORWARD TO ENJOYING THEIR DISAPPOINTMENT! THE TRAIN FROM THE EAST WILL NEVER ARRIVE!
WHO KNOWS WHAT HAPPENED AFTER THE BRIDGE COLLAPSED?
THOSE SUFFERING SQUEAKERS WILL HAVE CRASHED!
SHHH!
DON'T DOUBT MY PLAN!
WHEN STANFORD REALIZES IT COLLAPSED, I'LL OFFER HIM MY DIRIGIBLES AND I'LL BE RICH!
WE'LL BE RICH, YOU MEAN!
I'LL LET YOU DRIVE THE DIRIGIBLES, BUT ONLY BECAUSE I'M MAGNANIMOUS!
NOW LET'S GO GET A WHIFF OF THE SITUATION FROM CLOSER UP.

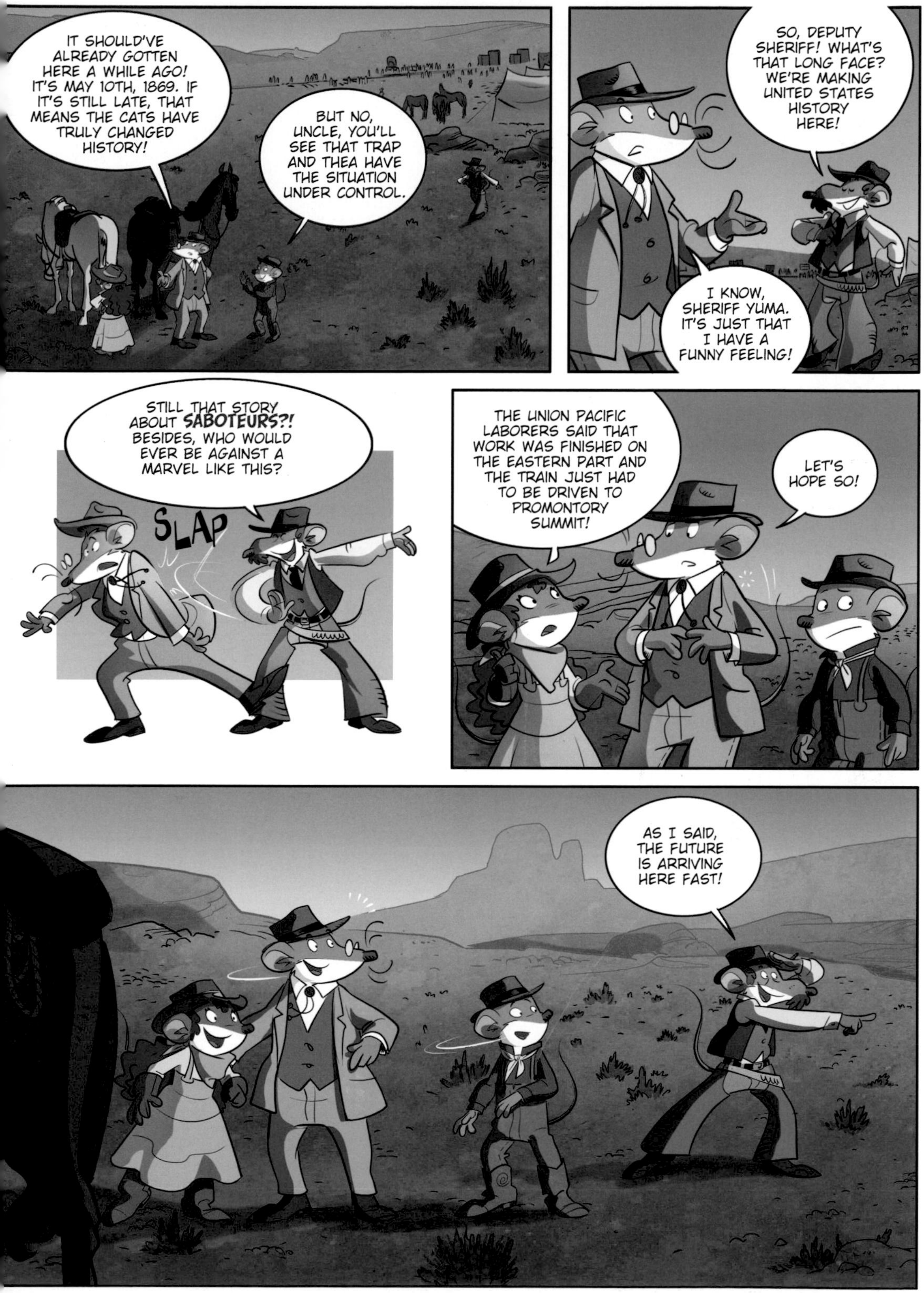

IT SHOULD'VE ALREADY GOTTEN HERE A WHILE AGO! IT'S MAY 10TH, 1869. IF IT'S STILL LATE, THAT MEANS THE CATS HAVE TRULY CHANGED HISTORY!
BUT NO, UNCLE, YOU'LL SEE THAT TRAP AND THEA HAVE THE SITUATION UNDER CONTROL.
SO, DEPUTY SHERIFF! WHAT'S THAT LONG FACE? WE'RE MAKING UNITED STATES HISTORY HERE!
I KNOW, SHERIFF YUMA. IT'S JUST THAT I HAVE A FUNNY FEELING!
STILL THAT STORY ABOUT SABOTEURS?! BESIDES, WHO WOULD EVER BE AGAINST A MARVEL LIKE THIS?
SLAP
THE UNION PACIFIC LABORERS SAID THAT WORK WAS FINISHED ON THE EASTERN PART AND THE TRAIN JUST HAD TO BE DRIVEN TO PROMONTORY SUMMIT!
LET'S HOPE SO!
AS I SAID, THE FUTURE IS ARRIVING HERE FAST!

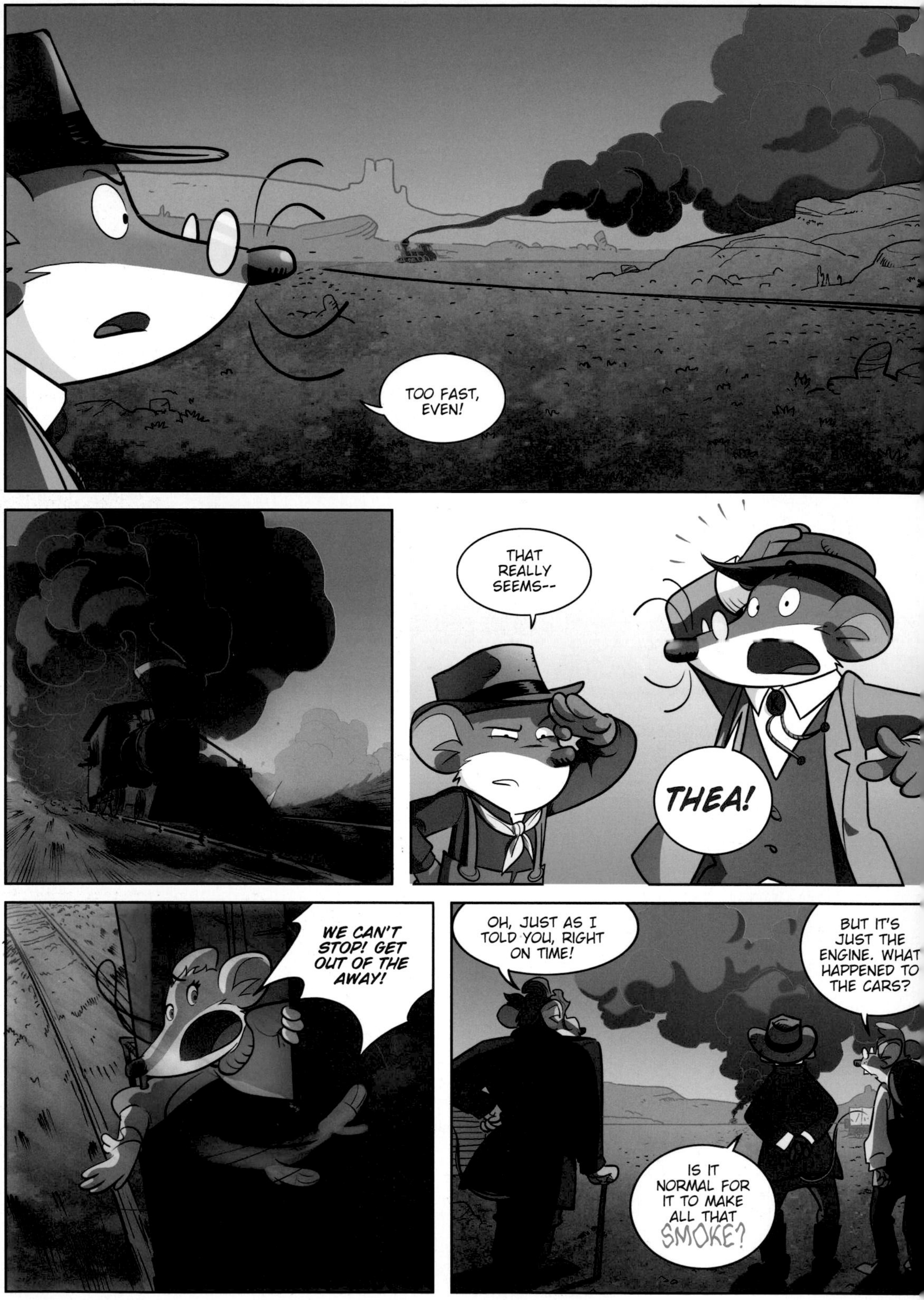
TOO FAST, EVEN!
THAT REALLY SEEMS--
THEA!
WE CAN'T STOP! GET OUT OF THE AWAY!
OH, JUST AS I TOLD YOU, RIGHT ON TIME!
BUT IT'S JUST THE ENGINE. WHAT HAPPENED TO THE CARS?
IS IT NORMAL FOR IT TO MAKE ALL THAT SMOKE?

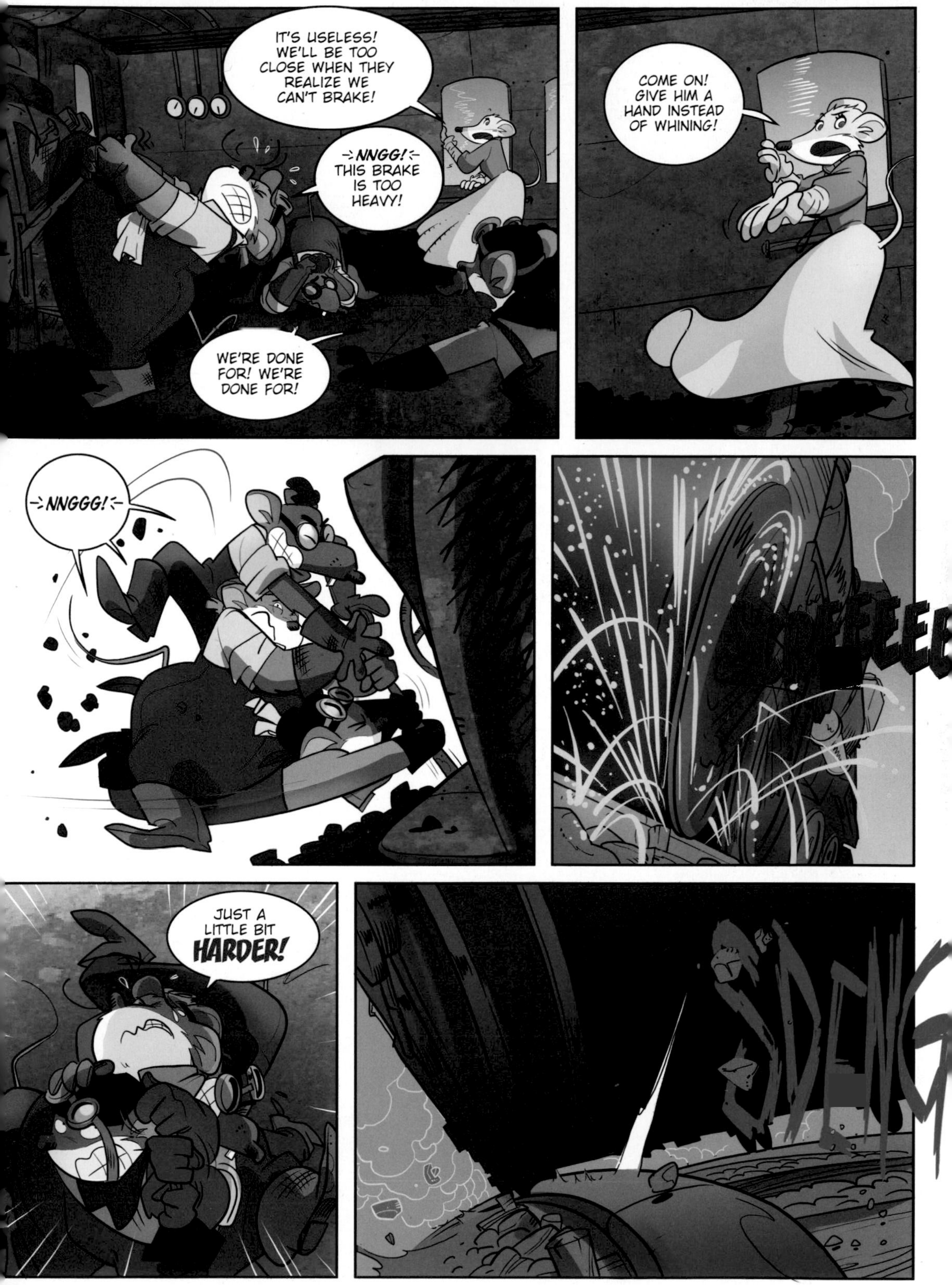
IT'S USELESS! WE'LL BE TOO CLOSE WHEN THEY REALIZE WE CAN'T BRAKE!
NNGG! THIS BRAKE IS TOO HEAVY!
WE'RE DONE FOR! WE'RE DONE FOR!
COME ON! GIVE HIM A HAND INSTEAD OF WHINING!
NNGGG!
JUST A LITTLE BIT HARDER!
SDENG

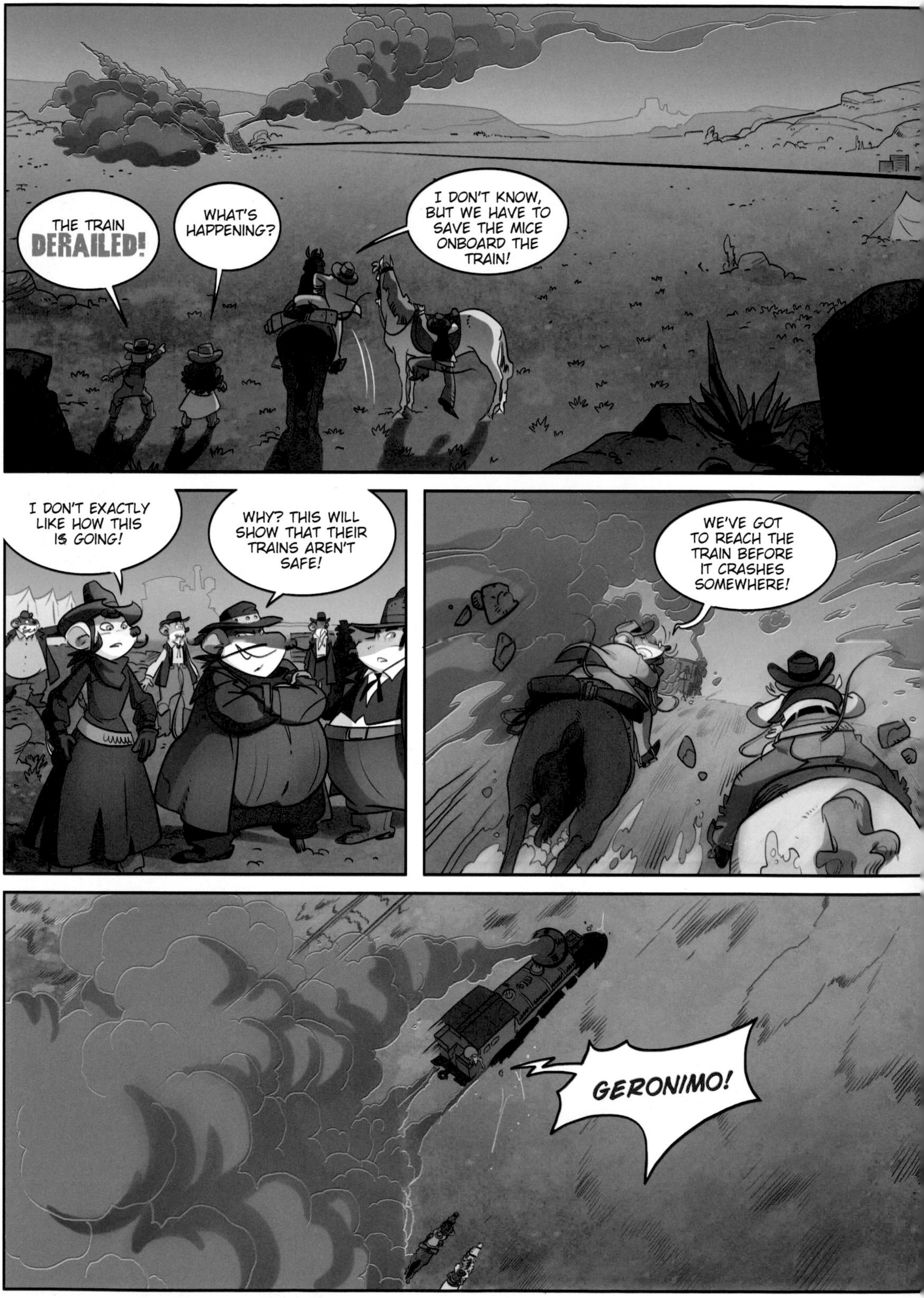
THE TRAIN DERAILED!
WHAT'S HAPPENING?
I DON'T KNOW, BUT WE HAVE TO SAVE THE MICE ONBOARD THE TRAIN!
I DON'T EXACTLY LIKE HOW THIS IS GOING!
WHY? THIS WILL SHOW THAT THEIR TRAINS AREN'T SAFE!
WE'VE GOT TO REACH THE TRAIN BEFORE IT CRASHES SOMEWHERE!
GERONIMO!

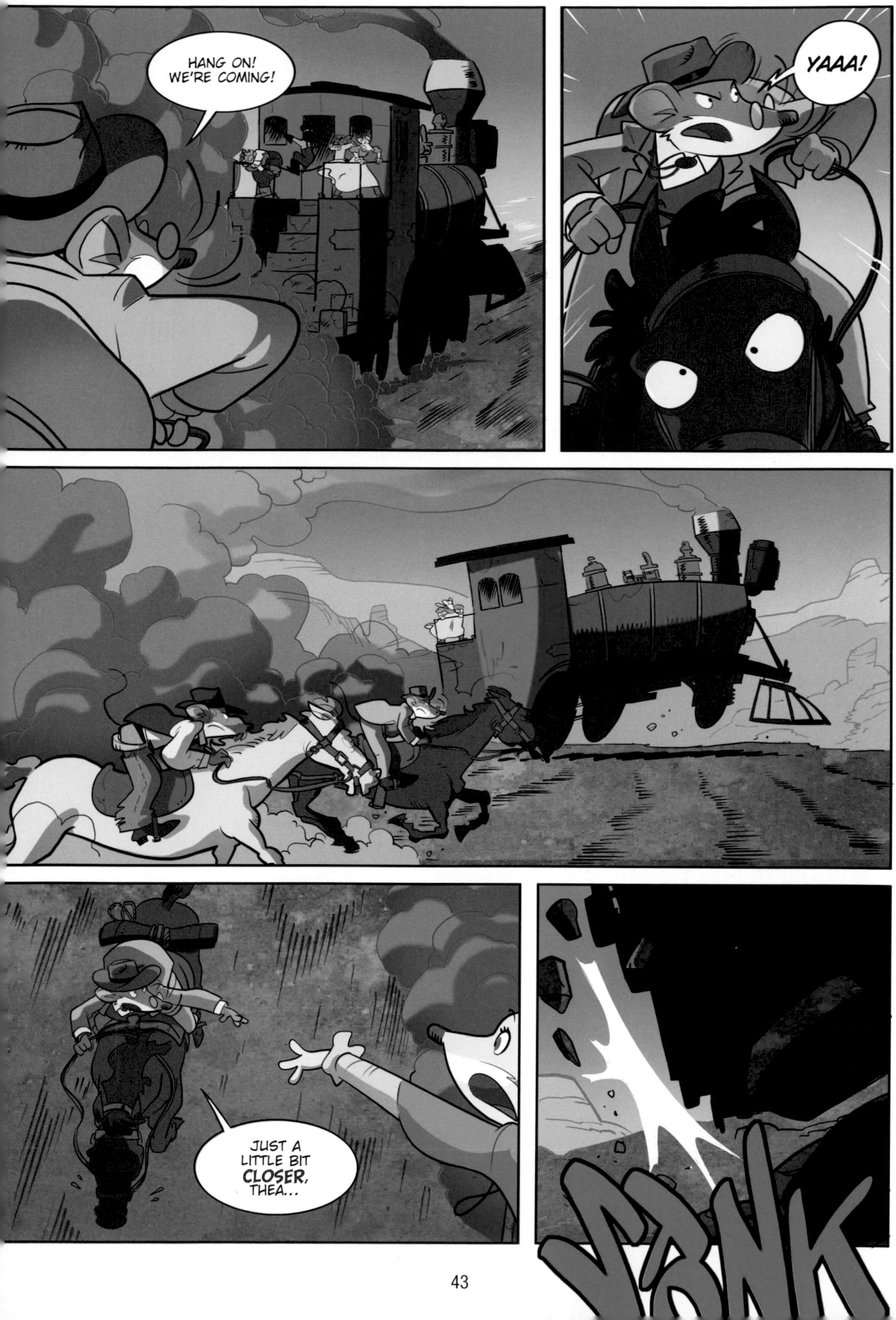
HANG ON! WE'RE COMING!
YAAA!
JUST A LITTLE BIT **CLOSER**, THEA...

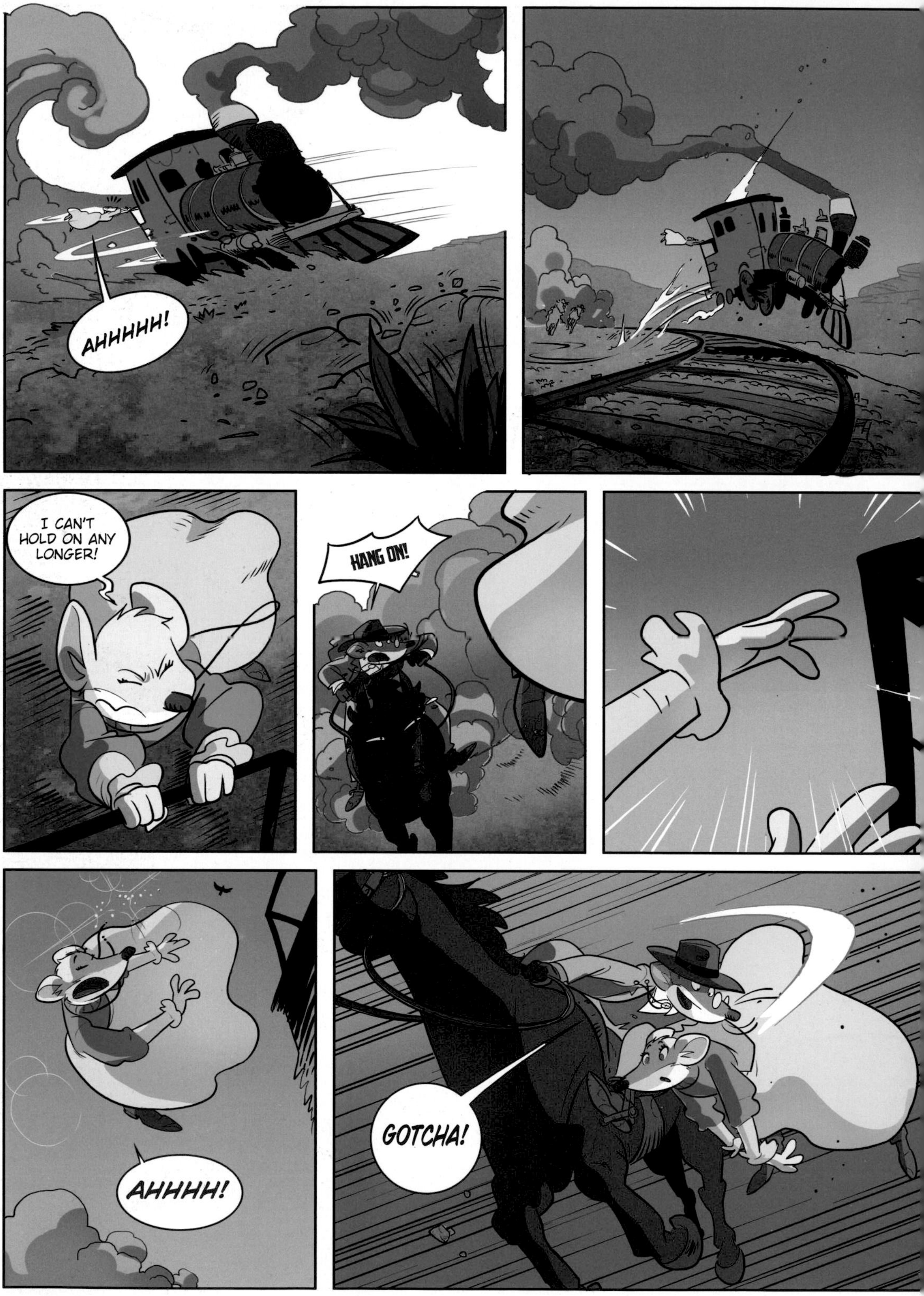
AHHHHH!
I CAN'T HOLD ON ANY LONGER!
HANG ON!
AHHHH!
GOTCHA!

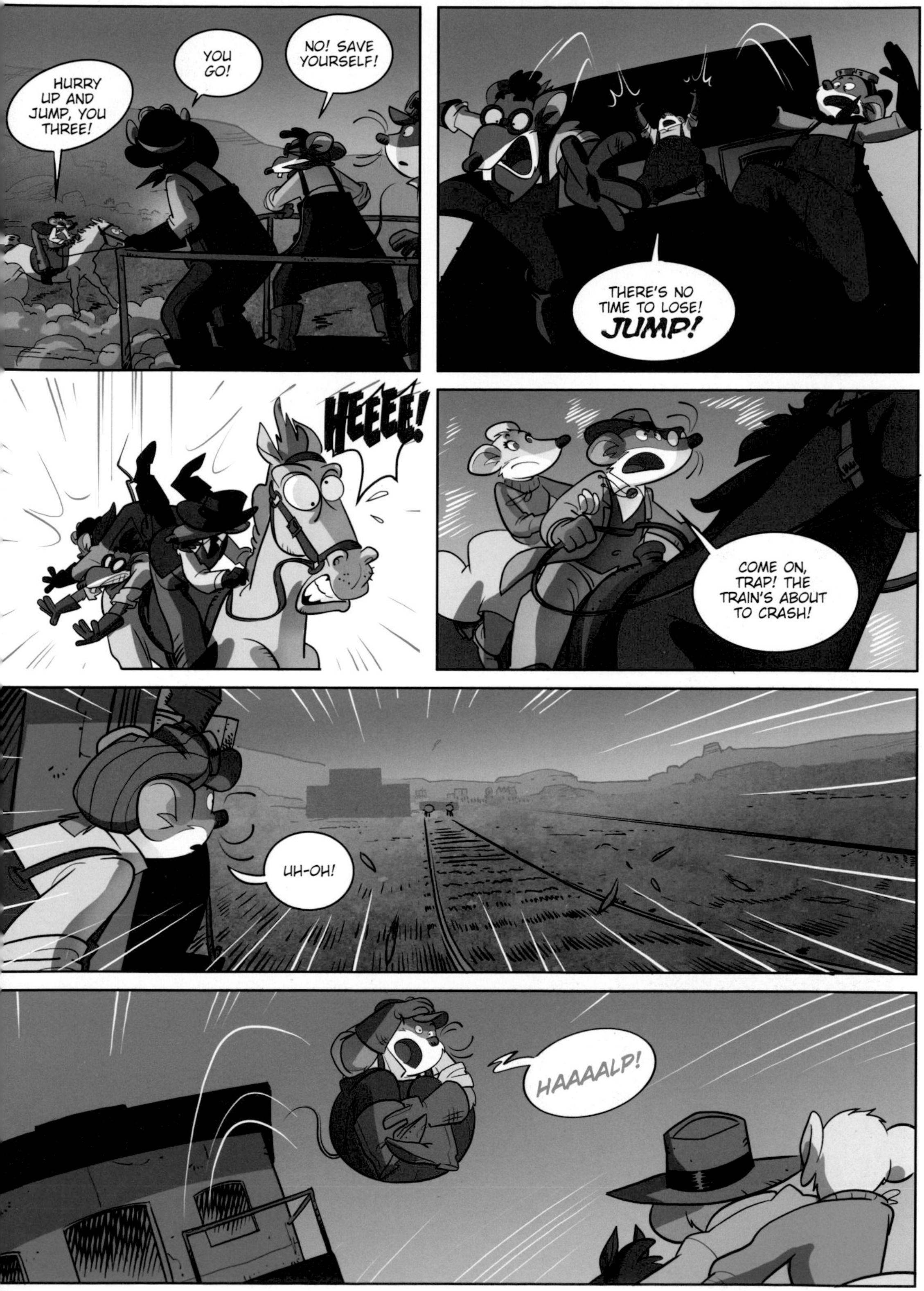
HURRY UP AND JUMP, YOU THREE!
YOU GO!
NO! SAVE YOURSELF!
THERE'S NO TIME TO LOSE! JUMP!
HEEEE!
COME ON, TRAP! THE TRAIN'S ABOUT TO CRASH!
UH-OH!
HAAAALP!

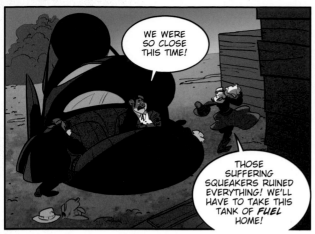

WE WERE SO CLOSE THIS TIME!

THOSE SUFFERING SQUEAKERS RUINED EVERYTHING! WE'LL HAVE TO TAKE THIS TANK OF *FUEL* HOME!

WELL, AT LEAST THIS TIME THERE ISN'T AN ANGRY MOB CHASING US!

BUT THERE'S A LOCOMOTIVE CHASING US...

AAAAHHH!

FLAMMABLE

AAAAHHH!

BOOOOOOMM

LOOK, UNCLE!

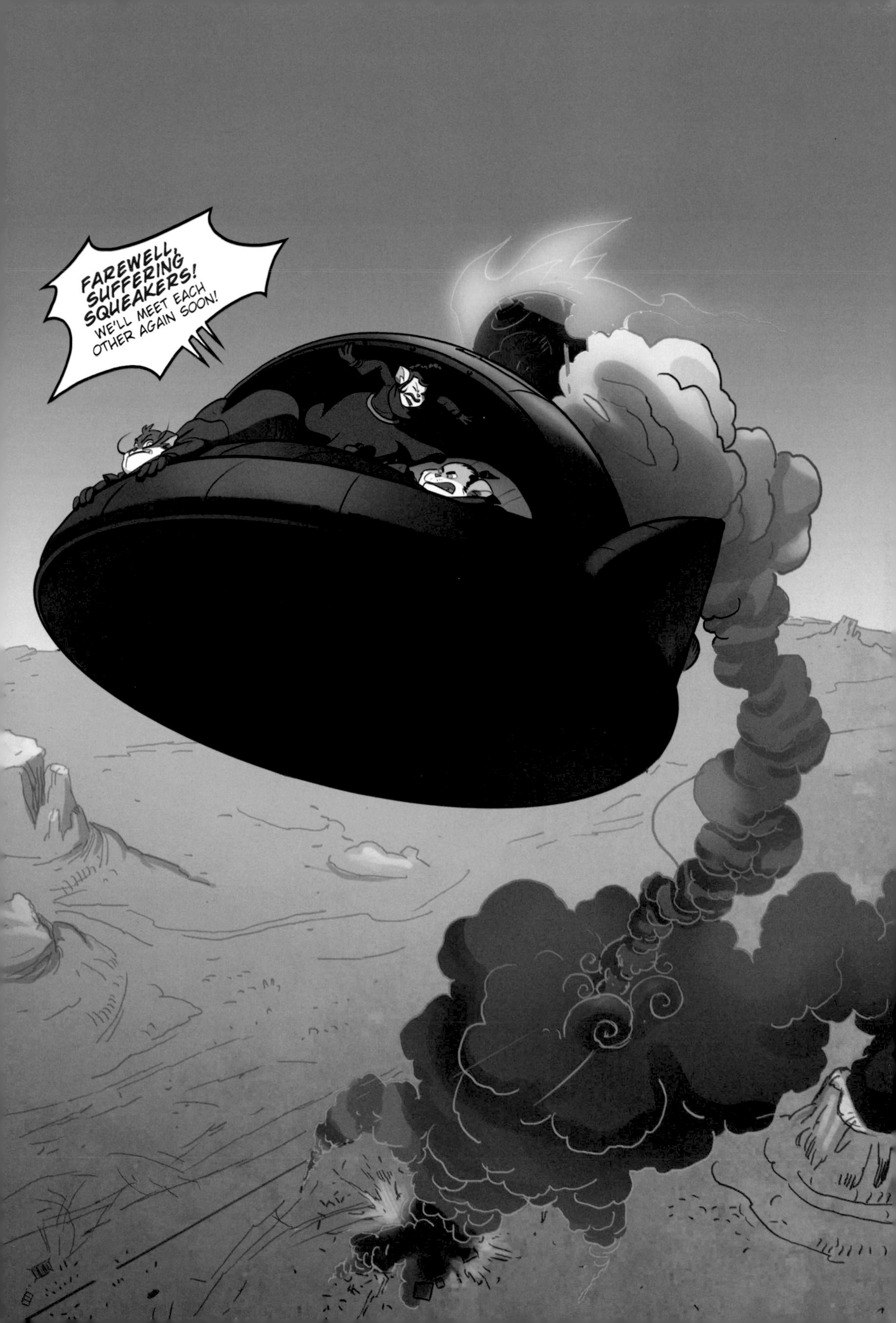
FAREWELL, SUFFERING SQUEAKERS! WE'LL MEET EACH OTHER AGAIN SOON!

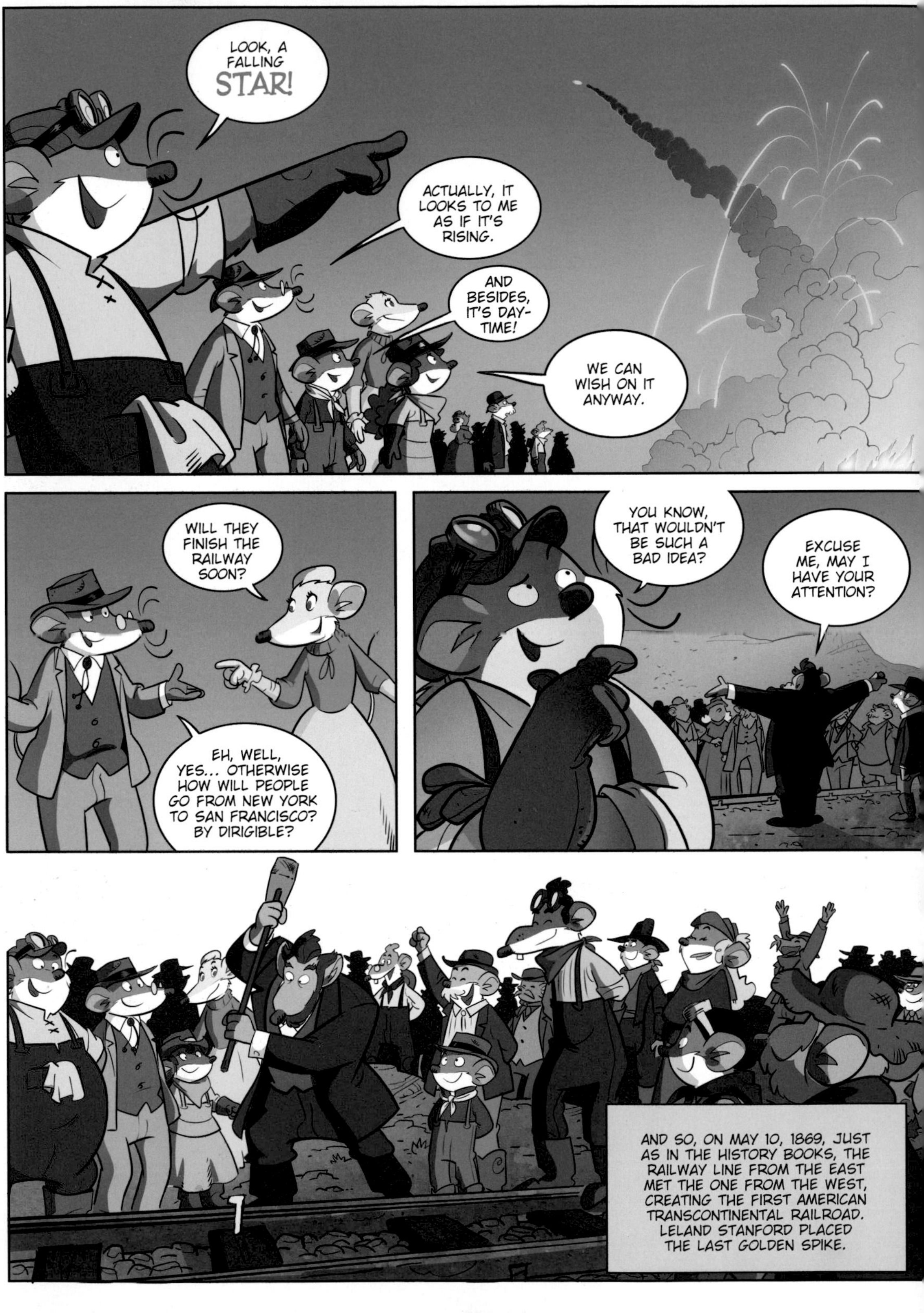
LOOK, A FALLING STAR!
ACTUALLY, IT LOOKS TO ME AS IF IT'S RISING.
AND BESIDES, IT'S DAY-TIME!
WE CAN WISH ON IT ANYWAY.
WILL THEY FINISH THE RAILWAY SOON?
EH, WELL, YES... OTHERWISE HOW WILL PEOPLE GO FROM NEW YORK TO SAN FRANCISCO? BY DIRIGIBLE?
YOU KNOW, THAT WOULDN'T BE SUCH A BAD IDEA?
EXCUSE ME, MAY I HAVE YOUR ATTENTION?
AND SO, ON MAY 10, 1869, JUST AS IN THE HISTORY BOOKS, THE RAILWAY LINE FROM THE EAST MET THE ONE FROM THE WEST, CREATING THE FIRST AMERICAN TRANSCONTINENTAL RAILROAD. LELAND STANFORD PLACED THE LAST GOLDEN SPIKE.

AT PRECISELY THAT MOMENT, A TELEGRAPH MESSAGE WAS SENT TO BOTH ENDS OF THE UNITED STATES, NEW YORK AND SAN FRANCISCO, TO SAY THAT WORK HAD BEEN COMPLETED...

...WHICH WAS CELEBRATED BY THE BELLS TOLLING.

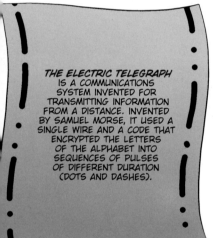

THE ELECTRIC TELEGRAPH IS A COMMUNICATIONS SYSTEM INVENTED FOR TRANSMITTING INFORMATION FROM A DISTANCE. INVENTED BY SAMUEL MORSE, IT USED A SINGLE WIRE AND A CODE THAT ENCRYPTED THE LETTERS OF THE ALPHABET INTO SEQUENCES OF PULSES OF DIFFERENT DURATION (DOTS AND DASHES).

ALL THAT REMAINED FOR US TO DO WAS SAY GOODBYE WHICH WAS MET WITH EVERYONE'S GRATITUDE...

COME ON, GERONIMO, WE'LL BE RUNNING IN JUST A FEW MINUTES!

THANKS, BUT AFTER ALL THAT ACTION, I COULD USE SOME PEACE AND QUIET!

COME ON, KIDS! OUR, ⇥AHEM⇤ RIDE, JUST ARRIVED!

WHIRR

WHIRR

WHIRR

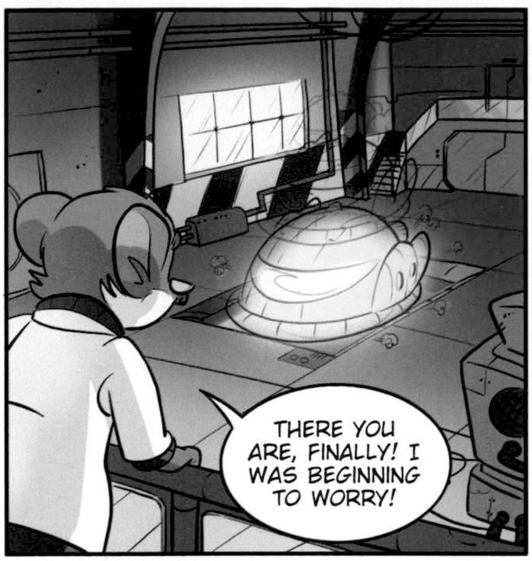
THERE YOU ARE, FINALLY! I WAS BEGINNING TO WORRY!

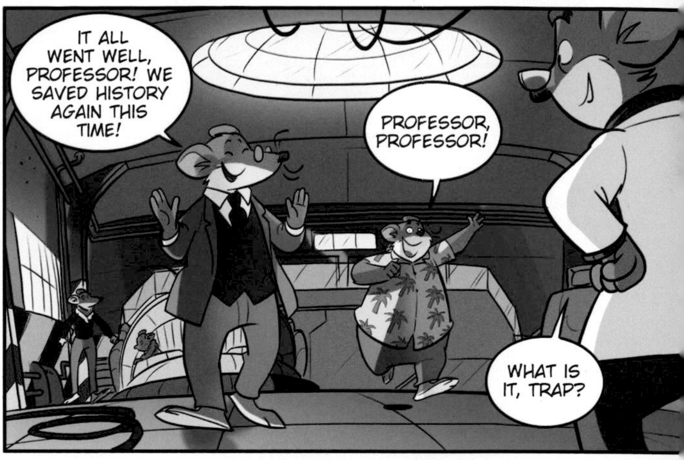
IT ALL WENT WELL, PROFESSOR! WE SAVED HISTORY AGAIN THIS TIME!
PROFESSOR, PROFESSOR!
WHAT IS IT, TRAP?

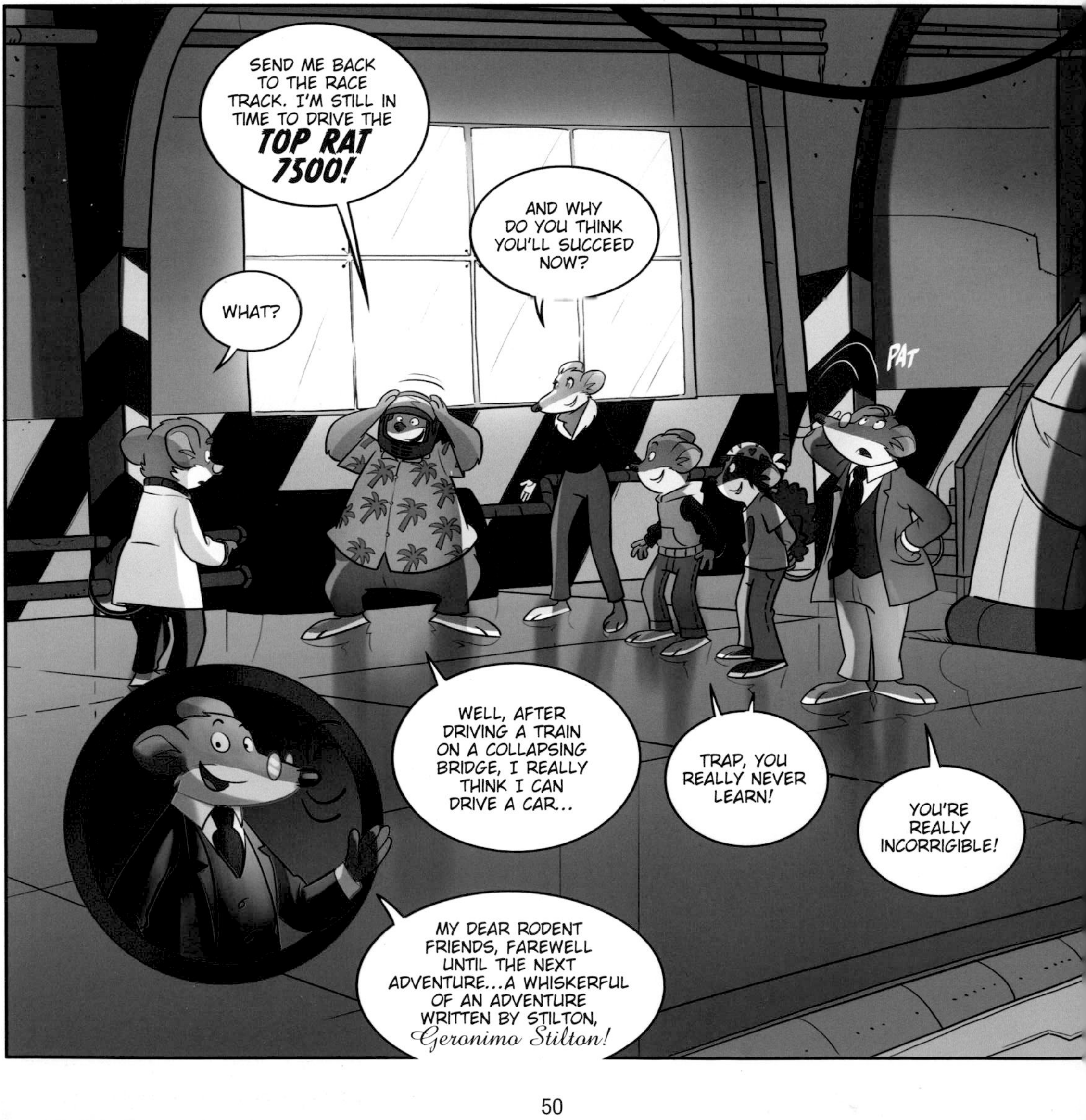
SEND ME BACK TO THE RACE TRACK. I'M STILL IN TIME TO DRIVE THE TOP RAT 7500!
WHAT?
AND WHY DO YOU THINK YOU'LL SUCCEED NOW?
PAT
WELL, AFTER DRIVING A TRAIN ON A COLLAPSING BRIDGE, I REALLY THINK I CAN DRIVE A CAR...
TRAP, YOU REALLY NEVER LEARN!
YOU'RE REALLY INCORRIGIBLE!
MY DEAR RODENT FRIENDS, FAREWELL UNTIL THE NEXT ADVENTURE...A WHISKERFUL OF AN ADVENTURE WRITTEN BY STILTON, Geronimo Stilton!

Watch Out For PAPERCUTZ

Welcome to the roughest, toughest, rootin', tootinist, thirteenth GERONIMO STILTON graphic novel from Papercutz, those East Coast city-slickers (even if Editor Michael Petranek is from Texas) dedicated to publishing great graphic novels for all ages. I'm Salicrup, *Jim Salicrup*, the Editor-in-Chief around these here parts. Even though I was born in The Bronx, I grew up around westerns. Allow me to explain…

NEW STORY! FULL-COLOR GRAPHIC NOVEL
THE HARDY BOYS
#12
DUDE RANCH O'DEATH
based on the series by Franklin W. Dixon
UNDERCOVER BROTHERS
Scott LOBDELL
Paulo HENRIQUE
PAPERCUTZ
© Simon & Schuster children's Publishing

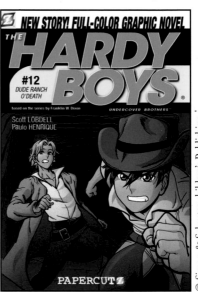

Back when I was just a youngin, there was only one TV set for my whole family. That meant we all had to share the same TV. And this was way before cable TV or 24-hour channels with nothing but cartoons (you guys don't know how lucky you are!). My mom liked to watch romantic shows, my dad and brother liked to watch action shows (which included lots of westerns, or as my dad called them, "Shoot 'em ups"!), and I enjoyed comedies. For better or worse, we all got to watch a lot of shows we may not have been all that interested in at the time, but in my case, I'm glad I got to watch so many great Western shows such as *Gunsmoke, Bonanza, The Wild, Wild, West, Wagon Train, The Rifle Man, Zorro,* and many more. There were even western comedies such as *F Troop* and *Rango*, and even western cartoons such as *The Lone Ranger* and *Yosemite Sam*, which I also loved.

Looking back, I think it's great that I was exposed to so many types of entertainment. As a result, even today I like a lot of variety—in movies, books, TV, music, food, and even in comics. Papercutz is proud to offer a great assortment of titles-- everything from ARIOL to LEGO® NINJAGO. But with exception of ZORRO and one HARDY BOYS graphic novel, we haven't published any westerns… until now (even if it does include time-traveling mice!). We hope you love "The Fastest Train in the West" as much as we do, and hope you'll be back for GERONIMO STILTON #14 "The First Mouse on the Moon." That'll be the first time Geronimo goes back into a time where I was actually alive! **MOLDY MOZZARELLA!** I'm getting really old! Check out the preview on the following pages.

See you in the future!

Jim

STAY IN TOUCH!

EMAIL:	salicrup@papercutz.com
WEB:	www.papercutz.com
TWITTER:	@papercutzgn
FACEBOOK:	PAPERCUTZGRAPHICNOVELS
FAN MAIL:	Papercutz, 160 Broadway, Suite 700, East Wing, New York, NY 10038

Caricature of Jim by Steve Brodner drawn at the MoCCA Art Fest.

Special preview of GERONIMO STILTON #14 “The First Mouse on the Moon”!

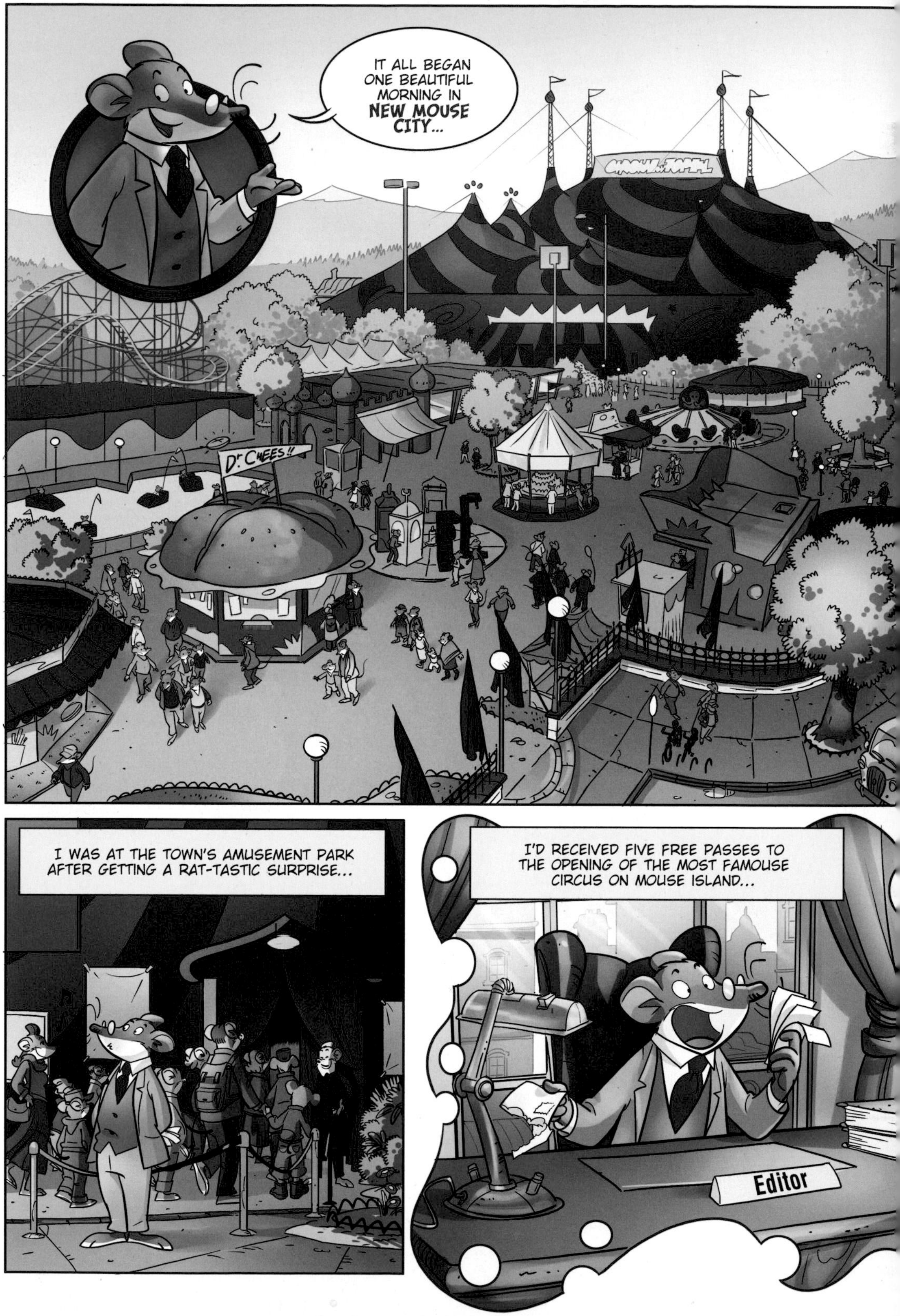

IT ALL BEGAN ONE BEAUTIFUL MORNING IN NEW MOUSE CITY...
I WAS AT THE TOWN'S AMUSEMENT PARK AFTER GETTING A RAT-TASTIC SURPRISE...
I'D RECEIVED FIVE FREE PASSES TO THE OPENING OF THE MOST FAMOUSE CIRCUS ON MOUSE ISLAND...
Editor

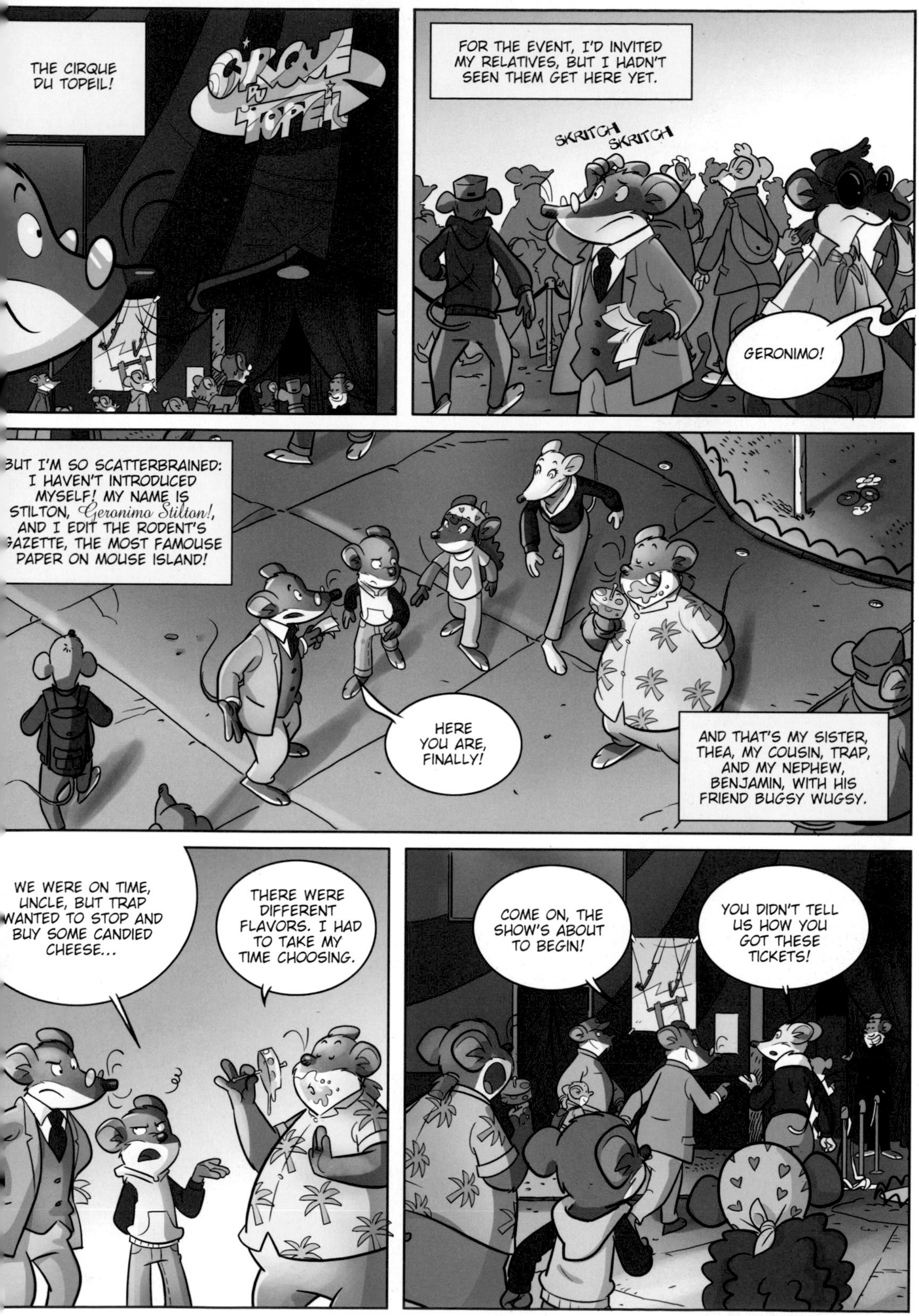
THE CIRQUE DU TOPEIL!
CIRQUE DU TOPEIL
FOR THE EVENT, I'D INVITED MY RELATIVES, BUT I HADN'T SEEN THEM GET HERE YET.
SKRITCH SKRITCH
GERONIMO!
BUT I'M SO SCATTERBRAINED: I HAVEN'T INTRODUCED MYSELF! MY NAME IS STILTON, *Geronimo Stilton!*, AND I EDIT THE RODENT'S GAZETTE, THE MOST FAMOUSE PAPER ON MOUSE ISLAND!
HERE YOU ARE, FINALLY!
AND THAT'S MY SISTER, THEA, MY COUSIN, TRAP, AND MY NEPHEW, BENJAMIN, WITH HIS FRIEND BUGSY WUGSY.
WE WERE ON TIME, UNCLE, BUT TRAP WANTED TO STOP AND BUY SOME CANDIED CHEESE...
THERE WERE DIFFERENT FLAVORS. I HAD TO TAKE MY TIME CHOOSING.
COME ON, THE SHOW'S ABOUT TO BEGIN!
YOU DIDN'T TELL US HOW YOU GOT THESE TICKETS!

IT'S A MYSTERY, REALLY! I GOT THEM FOR FREE IN AN ENVELOPE WITH NO RETURN ADDRESS...I THOUGHT IT MIGHT BE A GIFT FROM YOU!

MAYBE IT WAS A GIFT FROM THE CIRCUS AND THEY WANTED YOU TO WRITE AN ARTICLE ABOUT THEM!

SO WHY NOT SAY WHO THE SENDER WAS?

LET'S NOT THINK ABOUT THAT ANY LONGER. THE **SHOW'S** ABOUT TO BEGIN NOW!

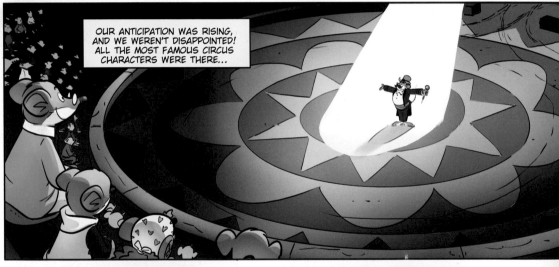

OUR ANTICIPATION WAS RISING, AND WE WEREN'T DISAPPOINTED! ALL THE MOST FAMOUS CIRCUS CHARACTERS WERE THERE...

THE CONTORTIONISTS...

AH, I DO THESE EXERCISES EVERY MORNING AS SOON AS I GET OUT OF BED!

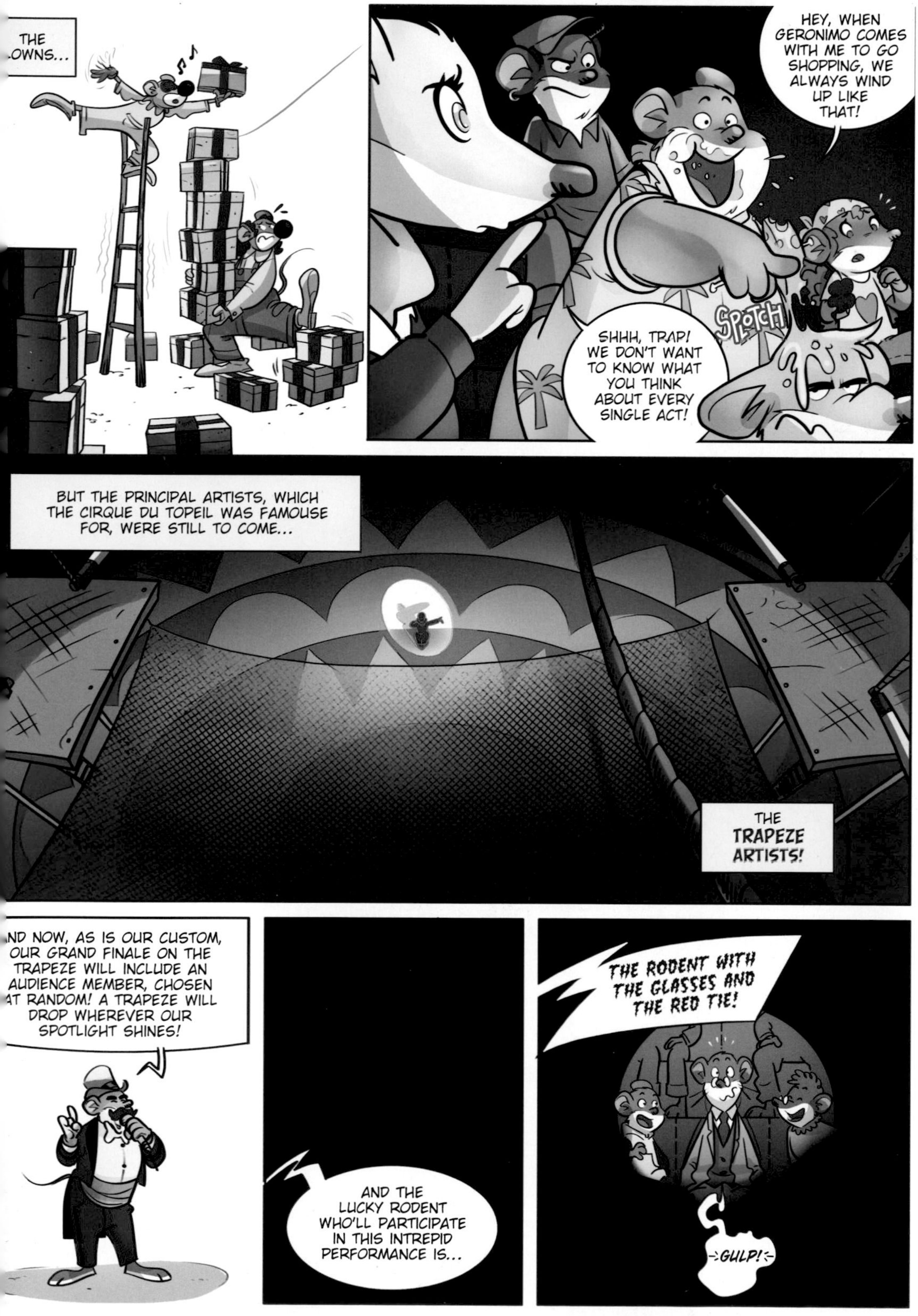

THE
.OWNS...
HEY, WHEN GERONIMO COMES WITH ME TO GO SHOPPING, WE ALWAYS WIND UP LIKE THAT!
SPLOTCH
SHHH, TRAP! WE DON'T WANT TO KNOW WHAT YOU THINK ABOUT EVERY SINGLE ACT!
BUT THE PRINCIPAL ARTISTS, WHICH THE CIRQUE DU TOPEIL WAS FAMOUSE FOR, WERE STILL TO COME...
THE TRAPEZE ARTISTS!
ND NOW, AS IS OUR CUSTOM, OUR GRAND FINALE ON THE TRAPEZE WILL INCLUDE AN AUDIENCE MEMBER, CHOSEN AT RANDOM! A TRAPEZE WILL DROP WHEREVER OUR SPOTLIGHT SHINES!
AND THE LUCKY RODENT WHO'LL PARTICIPATE IN THIS INTREPID PERFORMANCE IS...
THE RODENT WITH THE GLASSES AND THE RED TIE!
GULP!

n't miss GERONIMO STILTON #14 "The First Mouse on the Moon"!

Geronimo Stilton boxed sets! Three Graphic Novels collected in each box!

Available at booksellers everywhere.

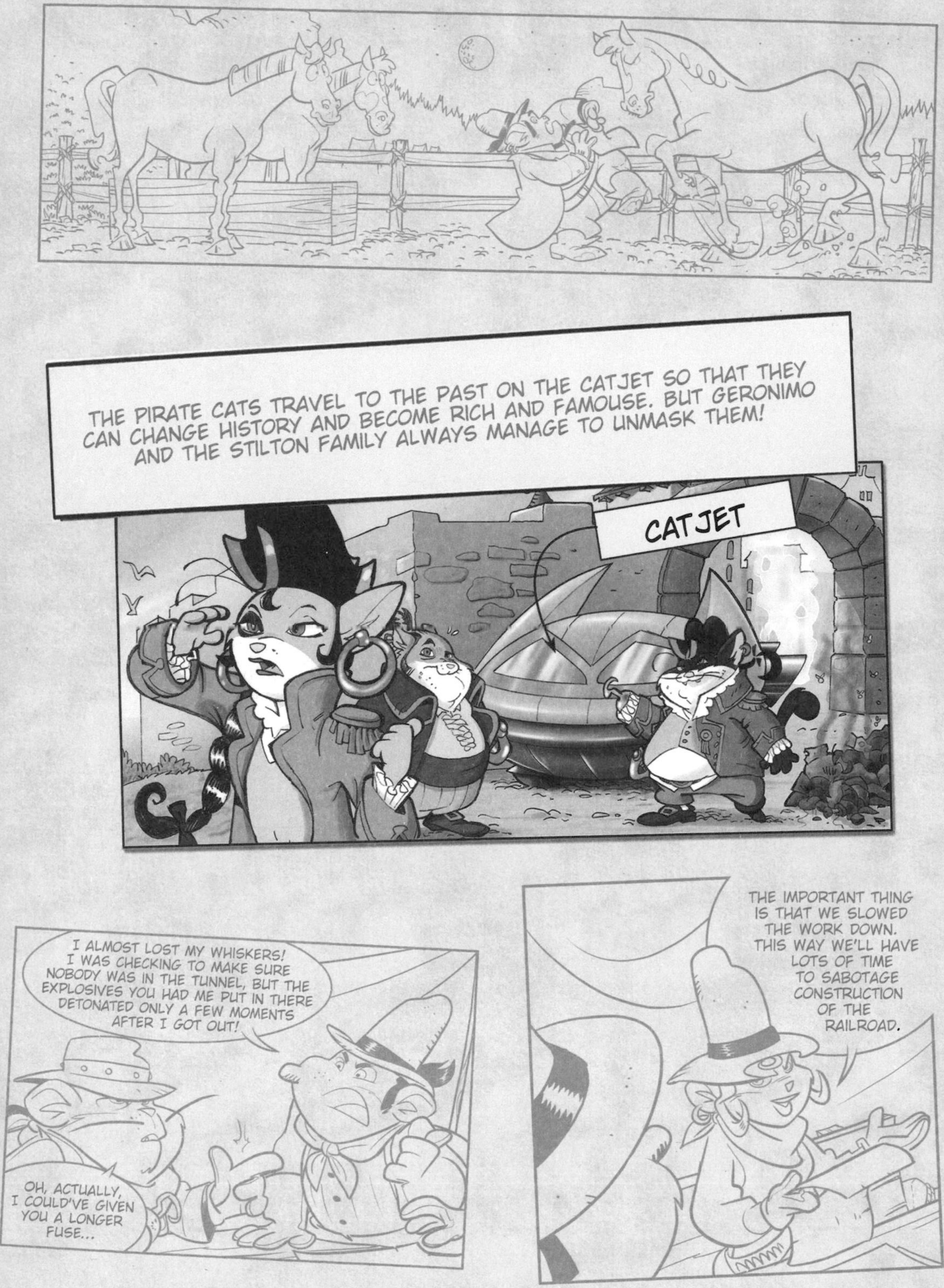
THE PIRATE CATS TRAVEL TO THE PAST ON THE CATJET SO THAT THEY CAN CHANGE HISTORY AND BECOME RICH AND FAMOUSE. BUT GERONIMO AND THE STILTON FAMILY ALWAYS MANAGE TO UNMASK THEM!
CATJET
I ALMOST LOST MY WHISKERS! I WAS CHECKING TO MAKE SURE NOBODY WAS IN THE TUNNEL, BUT THE EXPLOSIVES YOU HAD ME PUT IN THERE DETONATED ONLY A FEW MOMENTS AFTER I GOT OUT!
OH, ACTUALLY, I COULD'VE GIVEN YOU A LONGER FUSE...
THE IMPORTANT THING IS THAT WE SLOWED THE WORK DOWN. THIS WAY WE'LL HAVE LOTS OF TIME TO SABOTAGE CONSTRUCTION OF THE RAILROAD.